Books by Donna Jo Napoli

THE BRAVEST THING

JIMMY, THE PICKPOCKET OF THE PALACE

THE PRINCE OF THE POND:
OTHERWISE KNOWN AS DE FAWG PIN

SHARK SHOCK

SOCCER SHOCK

WHEN THE WATER CLOSES OVER MY HEAD

THE MAGIC CIRCLE

ZEL

On Guard

On Guard

For the Students of the Episcopal Academy—

Go for the gold!

Donna Jo Napoli

2-19-98

Donna Jo Napoli

DUTTON · NEW YORK

F
NAP

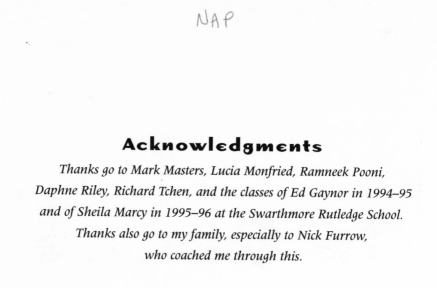

Acknowledgments

Thanks go to Mark Masters, Lucia Monfried, Ramneek Pooni,
Daphne Riley, Richard Tchen, and the classes of Ed Gaynor in 1994–95
and of Sheila Marcy in 1995–96 at the Swarthmore Rutledge School.
Thanks also go to my family, especially to Nick Furrow,
who coached me through this.

CIP Data is available.

Published in the United States by
Dutton Children's Books,
a division of Penguin Books USA Inc.
375 Hudson Street, New York, New York 10014
Jacket design by Semadar Megged
Interior design by Ellen M. Lucaire
Printed in U.S.A.   First Edition
ISBN 0-525-45759-3
1 3 5 7 9 10 8 6 4 2

This one's for Nick,
the Men's Foil Division II
National Champion for 1996

With love,
Mamma

Contents

Bombs 3

Cookbooks 13

Fun 19

Codes 27

Swords 37

Birthdays 49

The First Lesson 62

72 **Rafting**

84 **Strategy**

97 **Supper**

108 **The Fort**

118 **Rules and Rulers**

126 **Special**

138 **The Medal**

On Guard

Bombs

Mikey pedaled fast. The wind in his face felt great. He turned the corner and raced down the next block. He was flying.

His front tire hit a rock in the road and bounced high. Mikey jerked the handlebars as the bike came down. He swerved just enough to miss crashing into a parked car. Yes!

Raymond pulled up alongside Mikey. "Nice job."

"Thanks." Mikey was surprised. He hadn't realized Raymond was there. He smiled now in happy pride. Mikey had great balance, and that made him a great bike rider. He rode to the corner and stopped. This was where he turned. "Want to come play?"

"I can't. I've got to go work on my sound effects. Listen: Rrrrooom, rrrooom." Raymond paused and coughed three times. Then, "Rrrooom, rooom, rooom." He lifted his eyebrows. "That was a motorcycle with a faulty starter. The coughs were the part where the starter doesn't work."

"Good," said Mikey. "Real good."

"Motorcycles are easy. I want to learn something hard." Raymond waved and rode on.

Mikey understood. Mr. Gaynor, their fourth-grade teacher, was handing out one Olympic medal every Friday to the kid who was best at something that week. Raymond was determined his medal would be for sound effects. Raymond loved sounds.

Mikey loved weapons. Maybe he could win an Olympic medal for making a new weapon. Something original. Something no one else had ever even dreamed of.

The bus from the middle school stopped across the street. Mikey watched his big sister Victoria get off. He gave her a quick wave, zipped up his driveway, and ran into the house.

He dropped his backpack and bike helmet on the hall floor and raced upstairs to the playroom. He knew exactly what he was going to do. He had already made a stockpile of pinecones behind the garage. Pinecones looked a lot like hand grenades. But hand grenades were too small. Mikey would make something much more spectacular. He could fasten together about five or six pinecones into balls. They'd make great bombs. Original bombs.

Calvin sat on the playroom floor surrounded by wooden building blocks. "Hi, Mikey. Want to see my scab?" He stretched out his leg and pointed below the knee.

Mikey glanced at Calvin's scab. Then he looked again. "Hey, that's long. How'd you get it?"

"At recess. We have recess in kindergarten."

"I know. I remember." Mikey searched through the mess on the art shelf. Yes, there was the glue. He grabbed the bottle.

"See how big it is. It's the biggest scab I ever got."

Mikey picked the dried glue off the tip of the bottle. "Yeah. It's great." He turned the bottle upside down. The glue ran slowly down the sides. It was still good.

"Want to know the secret of my scabs?"

"Huh?" Mikey was in a rush. But it was always easier to get away from Calvin if he gave just that one extra minute of attention. "What's the secret?"

"They're really dirt."

"Huh? You can't call dirt a scab. That's dumb." Mikey ran down the stairs before Calvin could answer.

Victoria stood at the bottom of the stairs, hanging up her jacket. "Do you have a new friend?"

"Huh?"

"You were late coming home. Did you go to someone's house?"

"No."

"Too bad." Victoria's voice was singsongy. "I have a new friend."

"Oh. That's nice." Mikey ran past her out the back door. Yippy, their dog, looked up from a hole she was digging in the middle of the chrysanthemums. She barked happily and tagged at Mikey's heels as he went around behind the garage.

The pile of pinecones was a good foot high. Mikey picked out a big one. He squeezed a glob of glue on it and jammed another against it. This was going to be a fantastic bomb. He could almost feel the weight of the Olympic medal hanging around his neck already.

Yippy sniffed at the glue bottle. It tipped over.

Mikey quickly righted the bottle. The second pinecone fell off the instant he let go of it. The wet spot from the glue got covered with dirt. Mikey wiped it off with his shirt.

Yippy sniffed at the glue on Mikey's shirt. Then she licked it.

"Woof," said Mikey. "Stay away."

"Mikey?" called Calvin. "Where are you, Mikey?"

Mikey heard the screen door swing shut. Oh, no. Things had a way of going wrong when Calvin was around. Maybe if Mikey didn't answer, Calvin would go back inside. But just in case, he'd better hurry.

He lined up five pinecones, put globs of glue on the bottoms, and pressed them together. The points stuck out and looked scary. He clutched the whole thing to his chest. He knew he had to hold it tight for a few minutes to make the pinecones stick. He imagined standing on a rooftop and dropping the bomb on the enemy. It would fly apart on impact like shrapnel. "Boom," he said softly.

Yippy barked and bit the sticky clump on Mikey's shirt.

Mikey fended off the dog with his elbows.

"There you are." Calvin came around the corner of the garage. "Oh, you're gluing. I love to glue."

"Woof," said Mikey loudly. "Grrrrr."

Yippy barked and jumped at the pinecone bomb.

Mikey fell backward, with Yippy on top of him.

Calvin laughed and jumped up and down. His arms flapped like a bird's wings.

Mikey pushed the dog aside and stood up. "It's not funny, bird wing." He looked down at the stomped mess of glue and dirt that used to be his bomb. He turned around to scold Yippy, but the dog had settled under a bush, busily chewing away at the plastic glue bottle. Mikey sighed. "There goes the Olympics."

"What's the Olympics?"

"Nothing."

Calvin stood on one foot and held his arms out to each side. "Want to teach me how to ride my bike?"

"No." Mikey kicked at the pile of pinecones.

"You said you would. Last night." Calvin stared

solemnly at Mikey. "I'd teach you. If I was the big brother, I'd teach you."

Mikey sighed again. "All right, already. Get your bike."

Mikey, Victoria, and Calvin sat bent over sheets of paper at the kitchen table. Julie sat on the floor, ripping a piece of paper into little bits and stirring them into a bowl of water.

"Look." Calvin turned his paper to show what he had drawn.

Victoria frowned. "Is that water all around the house? You don't build houses in the middle of water."

"Water," said Julie. "In de water." She held up a spoonful of soggy paper bits. "Food in de water."

"You do if it's a moat," said Mikey. Still, Calvin's house did look like it was about to sink.

"It's Hamsterdam." Calvin pointed at the bottom of the house. "See? It's a boat. They live in boat houses."

"There's no such place as Hamsterdam," said Victoria.

"There is too. In kindergarten today we read a book about Hendrika. She's a cow. She fell in a canal."

"Amsterdam," said Mamma, as she walked through the kitchen. "That's a wonderful story." She carried a laundry basket full of dirty clothes. "Finish up your homework, Victoria and Mikey. Hurry now." She went downstairs to the basement.

"Amsterdam, of course," said Victoria. "It's the capital of Holland. Some people do live in houseboats there."

"Hamter food," said Julie. She put both hands into the bowl.

Calvin smiled. "I told you so." He turned his paper back around. "Have you ever been there?"

"Amsterdam? Of course not," said Victoria. "It's across the ocean."

Mikey turned to his homework again. "I only have three words left."

"You're so lucky," said Victoria. "Your homework is easy."

"It's not easy the way I do it. I put three spelling words in each sentence."

"I used to do that, too." Victoria pulled her braid over her shoulder and picked at the ends of it. "That's the only way to make it interesting."

Mikey tapped his pencil on the paper. "Give me a sentence with *planetarium, breathless,* and *fixture.*"

Victoria twisted her mouth. "There is no sentence with those three words."

"There has to be."

"Let me guess: Your class is going to a planetarium, isn't it?"

"It's part of our field trip to the Franklin Museum on Thursday."

"I knew it. Fourth-grade teachers are so predictable. I bet you've got words all about the sky in your spelling list."

Mikey looked down at the word *constellation*. He put one hand over the top of his paper so Victoria couldn't see. After all, Mr. Gaynor was a nice teacher. Mikey owed him that loyalty. "Just give me a sentence with those three words."

"Well, how about something deranged, like *'The bathroom fixture was shaped like a planetarium, so it left me breathless'?*"

"I can't write a sentence with *bathroom* in it."

"Of course you can. That's where you find fixtures."

"Everyone would laugh at me if I wrote *bathroom*."

Victoria sighed. "Fourth graders are so pathetic."

Mikey swallowed hard. "The sentence has to start with *M*, anyway, 'cause I already wrote an *M*."

"*Mikey* starts with *M*, right?" said Calvin. "*Calvin* starts with *C*. C-A-L-V-I-N."

Mamma came up the stairs. "That's right, Calvin. Very good. Bath time, everyone. And, Mikey, don't forget to pick up your bike helmet and put it in your cubby." Mamma scooped Julie into her arms and headed upstairs.

"I take showers now, Ma," called Victoria after her.

Lately Victoria had shifted to calling Mamma 'Ma.' Mikey felt odd every time she did it. Victoria stood up. "So it's not bath time for me. It's shower time." She gathered her papers. "Erase your *M*, Mikey. It's all messy, anyway."

"It's not messy. That's how I write."

"Just because you're left-handed doesn't mean you have to write like a monkey."

Mikey looked at his *M*. It wasn't so bad. Victoria just liked to pick on him. Like a chicken, picking at things in the chicken yard. "Kpok," said Mikey. "Kpok, kpok, kpok."

Victoria looked at him, stupefied. "You sound like a chicken."

"Kpok," said Mikey. "Someday I'll drop bombs in your bed."

"Bombs? Don't be ridiculous, Mikey." Victoria ran up the stairs.

Mikey gripped the pencil tight. He carefully wrote *My kitchen fixture was shaped like a planetarium, so it left me breathless.* He underlined *fixture, planetarium,* and *breathless.* Then he put everything away on the cupboard shelf that was his. Mamma called it his cubby, just like the cubby Mikey used to have in kindergarten when he was little. When he was as dumb and happy as Calvin. When he didn't have to worry about things like winning Olympic medals.

He climbed the stairs, pulling off his shirt as he went. Did he really write like a monkey?

Victoria deserved a bomb in her bed.

Only pinecone bombs weren't real bombs. Mikey needed to do something real. And he needed to do it well. Well enough to win the Olympic medal for it.

That would show Victoria.

Cookbooks

Mr. Gaynor cleared his throat. "We're not having guitar lessons in music class today."

"Let's do kazoos instead," said Stephen. "I'm good at kazoos."

"We're not going to music class at all." Mr. Gaynor smiled. "Instead, we're going to the library to do research."

Stephen groaned.

Research? Mikey had never done research. He leaned forward in his seat.

"What do we have to do research for?" asked Pete.

"All of you are going to do a research project on something you love and how it has changed through the ages."

"I can write about my little brother," said Jennifer Braid. "He's changed a lot through the ages."

There were three Jennifers in the class: Jennifer B., Jennifer M., and Jennifer S. Mikey had dubbed them Jennifer Braid, Jennifer Mouth, and Jennifer Snot.

Jennifer Braid had a long braid, of course. Jennifer Mouth never talked, but she did have a pretty mouth. And Jennifer Snot had a cold, and it was still as hot as summer.

Mr. Gaynor shook his head. "It's got to be something that's been around a lot longer than your brother."

Guns, thought Mikey. Of course. Guns had changed a lot over the years.

"It takes time to do research," said Mr. Gaynor. He sat on the edge of his desk and leaned forward. "That's why we're going to the library now to get books. You'll have till the end of October to do the project. Between now and then, read your books and talk to your parents about your ideas."

Parents? Oh, no. Mamma hated guns.

Pete waved his hand. "Can I do it on candy?"

"Sure, candy's a great idea."

Candy was a great idea. Mikey perked up. There were plenty of things he loved besides guns. Like baseball. Mikey was a good pitcher. He had great aim. "Can I do it on baseball?"

"Baseball hasn't been around long enough. You want something that goes back at least a thousand years."

"How do we know what goes back a thousand years?" asked Jennifer Braid.

"You don't yet. That's why you need to do research." Mr. Gaynor swung his legs. "Whoever does the best research project will get the Olympic medal that week."

A half hour later Mikey stood in line at the librarian's checkout desk. The books he held were weighty. They were about food all around the world. Mikey was going to do his research project on cooking because his parents always said he was a superb cook. Cooking was a foolproof way to win an Olympic medal.

Mikey set the books on the desk and pushed them along with him as the line moved ahead. He had already chosen the recipe he would try first: stuffed baked cucumbers. It was Chinese.

"What're you doing with those books?"

Mikey turned around and faced Bill. "Huh?"

"Food books." Bill wrinkled his nose. "Sort of like cookbooks." His cheeks were beefy red, his hair was white blond, and he was sort of chubby. Mr. Gaynor seemed to like him. In fact, Mr. Gaynor had awarded the first Olympic medal of the year to Bill. It said, "1st Prize—R." The R stood for *readiness.* It hung around Bill's neck on a ribbon, and Bill was pulling on it right now.

But Mikey wasn't so sure about Bill. Bill's family had just moved to town and all Mikey really knew about Bill was that he talked loud. Mikey looked down. Maybe if he acted like he was thinking about something else, Bill would forget all about him.

"The closest I've ever been to cooking," said Bill, talking louder, "was lunchtime at camp. I made mustard sandwiches every day."

Mikey looked up. "Mustard sandwiches?"

"Yeah, cheese and mustard."

"That sounds good."

Bill rubbed his stomach, as though enjoying the memory. "They were. They were delicious 'cause the cheese tasted like nothing."

Mikey liked cheese.

"But real cooking, that's different. I bet no other boys are going to choose cookbooks."

Suddenly Mikey picked up his cookbooks and walked to the shelves he'd gotten them from. He shoved them back into place. His throat felt tight. He wasn't sure Bill was calling him a sissy, but it wasn't worth finding out.

He walked to a different section of the library, sat on the floor, and picked a book off the shelf at random. This one turned out to be on boats.

Mikey didn't love boats. But he needed a research project. He opened the book. A picture of a schooner in the middle of the ocean stared back at him. Water wasn't Mikey's favorite thing. He had learned to swim just last summer—and he was okay at it. But not good enough to feel safe in a boat in the middle of the ocean. He turned the page quickly and read about Eskimo umiaks.

Mr. Gaynor came striding into the library. "Okay, class," he called softly. "Library time is over. If you haven't already checked out your books, do it fast. Then form a line silently." He held up his right hand, and Jennifer Snot quickly got into line first. Jennifer Snot loved to be first at everything.

Within minutes almost everyone in the class was in line, each one holding just the right books for their projects.

Mikey looked again at the book in his hands. His heart sank, but there was no time to pick anything else now. He took the book over to the librarian's desk. He waited while Mrs. Rowe, the librarian, typed something into her computer.

Bill came up behind him again. Bill seemed to pop up behind Mikey every time Mikey did anything. He peered over Mikey's shoulder. "Boats? You love boats?"

Mikey shrugged.

"I like boats, too." Bill moved up alongside Mikey. He smiled. "That gives me an idea." He paused.

Mikey was about to ask what Bill's idea was when he glanced at the books Bill was holding. "Hey, those are the cookbooks."

"Yeah. Why'd you put them back?"

"I thought . . . I don't know."

"Well, I'm glad you did." Bill smiled down at his books. "I love desserts." He gave a little laugh and rubbed his stomach like he'd done before. "I guess you can tell."

Mikey clutched his boat book so tight his fingers hurt. Nothing was going right. Bill had the books that Mikey really wanted. And Mikey had a boat book. A yucky boat book. He felt slightly woozy, almost as though he were seasick. He imagined an Olympic medal falling into the ocean, sinking, sinking, sinking.

Mikey walked in the front door. "Hello," he called out, yanking at the strap of his bike helmet.

Their bird, Dragon, sang out from his cage, as if in greeting. Mikey whistled to Dragon.

Calvin came running up the stairs from the basement. "Hi, Mikey." His hands were grimy, and there was dirt smeared across one cheek. "Me and Mamma are shoveling."

"Shoveling in the basement?"

"I turned over a board and wiggly things ran out." Calvin jumped in a circle. "Mamma screamed."

"Mikey," called Mamma right then. "Can you help me? I've got two big garbage cans to carry out to the driveway."

Mikey whistled to Dragon again. Dragon was a parakeet. Mikey had named him Dragon when they first got him because he was all green. Victoria had said that was the worst name she'd ever heard for a bird. But it had stuck—and Mikey was glad it had stuck. Dragon's name was one of Mikey's triumphs over Victoria.

Most of the time Dragon was full of songs. Right now Dragon's song was almost sweet enough to make Mikey forget about his boat book. He put his backpack and helmet in his cubby. Then he went down the basement stairs.

"Can you believe this mess?" Mamma looked all around, but she didn't seem upset. She seemed kind of happy. "This place has been flooded so many times, at the edges the floor was three inches deep with mud. I can't believe I've let it stay this way so long."

Mikey took one handle of a garbage can and tried to pull it. It was heavy. "Why're you cleaning it out, anyway?"

Mamma took the other handle. "I'm not just cleaning. I'm going to pound the accumulated lime off the walls with a hammer . . ."

"I'm going to help," said Calvin. "I get to pound. Kindergarteners can pound."

"And then I'm going to cement up the cracks and Thoro-seal the walls." Mamma panted as they lugged the garbage can up the steps. "I got a book from the library on how to waterproof basements. Last of all, I'll wash and paint the floor."

Calvin raced past Mamma and opened the door.

Mamma and Mikey carried the garbage can out to the driveway and set it down. "Just one more can, Mikey."

"Sure, Mamma." Mikey looked at Mamma's sweaty face. "Why're you doing all this?"

"It'll be a playroom," said Mamma. "It doesn't make sense for our basement to be nothing but a place for the washer and dryer. And if it stays dry after the first heavy rain, I'll even put a carpet on the playroom floor."

"My playroom," said Calvin.

"Everyone's playroom, dirt cheek," said Mikey to Calvin.

Mikey and Mamma carried out the second can of muck. It was just as heavy as the first. "I need a shower," said Mamma. "I'm all sticky and stinky."

"Paul threw up in kindergarten today," said Calvin. "That was sticky and stinky."

"Yuck," said Mikey.

Mamma pushed her hair out of her face. "This is sort of fun, you know? It feels good to get tired from hard labor." She smiled. "Thanks, boys." Then she went upstairs.

Mikey suddenly remembered his research project. The sooner he started it, the sooner it would be over. And the sooner it was over, the sooner he'd be able to forget all about boats and turn his attention back to winning that Olympic medal. "I've got work to do," he said.

"Work?" Calvin stood beside him. "You just got home. Let's play catch."

"You can't catch," said Mikey.

Calvin reached into his pocket and took out a giant pretzel. "Here." He gave it to Mikey. "I saved it for you. Mamma was about to finish the whole box, but I saved you that one."

Mikey loved pretzels. He wiped it off and ate it. "All right. We can play catch for a little while." He went to his cubby and got out his baseball and glove. Then he headed out the kitchen door with Calvin at his heels.

"You ready?"

Calvin nodded. He squeezed his eyes shut and thrust his hands forward.

"Open your eyes, Calvin."

Calvin opened his eyes.

"I've told you a zillion times: You can't catch with your eyes closed. I'll throw it easy, okay?"

Calvin nodded. "Okay."

Mikey tossed the ball.

Calvin shut his eyes, and the ball hit him in the chest. He opened his eyes and ran to get the ball. He threw it. It went over Mikey's head and bounced across the driveway, plopping into the raspberry brambles.

Mikey got down on his hands and knees and reached his arm carefully under the thorny canes. "Got it." He stood up. "Ready?" He tossed the ball again.

Calvin shut his eyes and waved his hands over his head. The ball hit him in the arm. He opened his eyes and ran after it.

"Look, Calvin. I think you should do something else."

Calvin picked up the ball and threw it wildly. It slammed against the side of the garage.

Mikey got the ball. "Go practice on your bike." He threw the ball up and caught it in his mitt.

"Will you help me?"

"No. I've got to get to work."

Calvin pulled on the hem of his T-shirt. "I can't do it without you."

"Then ride your tricycle."

Mikey threw the ball up in the air and caught it again. He watched Calvin come riding out of the garage on the old tricycle, which had been new with Victoria, semi-beat-up with Mikey, and now totally a wreck with Calvin. Poor Julie. By the time she got it, it probably wouldn't have any wheels left.

Calvin smiled. "You catch good."

Mikey wished Calvin hadn't said that. Calvin was always saying things to make Mikey feel guilty.

"And you pass good, too."

"Passes are in football," said Mikey.

"You throw good. That's what I meant. And you run fast."

It was true. Mikey was quick on his feet. If Calvin kept up the flattery, Mikey would have to give him a bike lesson.

The kitchen door opened. Yippy bounded out with Julie right behind, holding her rag doll by the arm. Mamma leaned out the door. Her wet hair dripped on the shoulders of her robe. "Julie woke up. Watch her while I get dressed, will you, Mikey?" She took the rag doll from Julie. "Let me put this away while you play, okay?" Then she looked back at Mikey. "And no throwing that ball while Julie's around." Mamma closed the door.

Calvin got off his tricycle. "You have to put the ball away. Want to wrestle?"

"I'm twice your size, Calvin. I'm bigger than you than Victoria is than me."

"What?" said Calvin.

"We can't wrestle."

"Yes, we can. I love to wrestle," said Calvin. He grabbed Yippy around the neck and fell to the ground with her.

Julie laughed. "Jump baby dog." She flung herself on top of Calvin and Yippy.

Mikey tossed the ball in the air and caught it. Then he thought about how Mamma would scold him for doing that around Julie. "Let's all go inside. Come on, I've got things to do."

Calvin disentangled himself from Julie and Yippy. "What are we going to do?"

"Not we—me. My research project."

"What's that?"

"It's some dumb thing about boats."

"I love boats," said Calvin. "Boats bash into each other."

"In wars. Only we can't even play war because Mamma doesn't let us point guns. Mamma doesn't let us do anything fun." Mikey thought about an enemy stalking into their yard right now and killing him and Calvin and Julie. Then Mamma would be sorry she never let them learn warfare.

"You can use seeds," said Calvin.

"Seeds? What for?"

Calvin dug around in his pocket. He brought out a handful of sunflower seeds. He threw one on the ground. "Boom!" He laughed. "Seeds are good for war."

"Calvin, that's the dumbest thing I ever heard. You get dumber every day." First Mamma thought cleaning the garage was fun; now Calvin thought throwing seeds instead of shooting guns was fun.

Julie picked up the seed. "Boom!" she screamed. She ran over and kissed Mikey on the arm. "Boom, boom, boom."

Everyone in this family was crazy.

Codes

Mikey sat on the bedroom floor and wrote carefully in fluorescent purple crayon. He carried the piece of paper over to the mirror on the closet door. The warm glow of satisfaction filled him. Maybe this project was going to be fun, after all.

"Dinnertime," said Calvin, galloping into the room. "What're you doing, Mikey?"

"It's a secret code." Mikey showed the paper to Calvin.

"I love secrets." Calvin touched it gently. "Is it magic?"

"Uh-uh. It says something, but only I know what."

"What use is a code only you know?" Victoria stood in the doorway.

"You shouldn't eavesdrop," said Mikey.

"I wasn't eavesdropping. Mamma said to get you for dinner."

"You were spying," said Mikey.

"Who would want to spy on you? Besides, I have better things to do." She tossed her braid over her shoulder.

"Like what?"

"Like finding a newspaper article for my current-events paper." Victoria leaned over Calvin's shoulder and looked at the paper. "Hmmm. That's a mirror code, isn't it?"

Mikey snatched the paper from Calvin and folded it.

"It says SHIPS," said Victoria. "All you have to do is hold it up to the mirror, and you can read it."

"You saw me, spy face."

"No, I didn't. It's obvious."

Pick pick pick, thought Mikey. "Kpok, kpok." He stuck the paper in his pocket. "If we were on a ship, I'd never write you a note in code, even if you were dying."

"But you'd write to me, wouldn't you, Mikey?" Calvin tugged on Mikey's arm. "I love codes."

"Why would I want a note in code if I was dying?" Victoria put a hand on her hip. "You're losing your mind."

"Dinner!" called Mamma from the dining room.

"You'd make a horrible pirate," said Mikey. "Calvin would be a zillion times better than you."

"Goody." Calvin slapped his chest with both hands. "I get to be a pirate." He marched around

Victoria. "And Dragon can be our parrot. He can tell us where the treasures are."

"Dragon can't even talk," said Victoria. "I'm going back to my current events paper. It's all about moon glow."

"Moon glow," murmured Calvin. "Oh, it's about moon glow."

"That's right," said Victoria. "Scientists just discovered that the light of the full moon causes the earth to heat up. Only a little bit—just point zero three degrees."

Mikey didn't know what "point zero three degrees" meant. Victoria was showing off. "The moon isn't good for anything."

"Yes, it is," said Calvin. "The moon's a lot more useful than the sun, 'cause it shines at night when you need it."

"Calvin!" Victoria looked shocked. "That is so illogical, I can't even begin to explain. You're hopeless. Both of you."

"Last call," said Mamma. "Come down or starve."

"Pass the peas, please," said Daddy. He looked meaningfully at Calvin. "Calvin, what letter did I use over and over at the beginning of the words? Listen again: *Pass the peas, please.*"

Calvin looked intently at Daddy. He put his lips together and mouthed the words slowly. *"P?"*

"You got it." Daddy smiled. "Good work."

"I love *P*," said Calvin. "*Pink* starts with *P*."

"*Pirate* starts with *P*," said Mikey.

Victoria looked at Mikey. "Unless you're deranged and spell it backward in a secret code."

Mikey took a gulp of milk. He imagined Victoria in a duel, swords flashing, backed to the edge of the ship, about to get her head cut off. He'd probably have to be the one to come to her rescue. "A terrible pirate, spy face," he said softly.

"But I'll be a good pirate," said Calvin.

Victoria lifted her chin.

"So, Victoria," said Daddy quickly, looking anxiously from Mikey to Victoria, "what did you learn in school today?"

"You can't ask a sixth grader a question like that." Victoria put a ring of purple onion on her hamburger. "We don't learn things in one day. We work on them over time."

Daddy chewed his hamburger thoughtfully. "So what are you working on?"

"Countries." Victoria spread spicy brown mustard on her bun. "We each got a country to study. Mine's Ireland. I have to learn about everything Irish. Then I'll give a class report."

"Eat," said Julie. She put her finger on a pea and squashed it. "Eat pea." She searched around her plate. "Pea all gone. Eat bun." She squished her bun in her fingers.

Mikey expected Mamma to tell Julie not to play with her food. But Mamma just kept eating. Mikey put some peas from his plate onto Julie's. Then he ate potato salad. He had made it just right—with lots of diced celery and onions. It really was a shame he wasn't doing his research project on cooking.

Julie dropped her squished bun. "Yippy," she called.

Yippy bounded out from under the table and pounced on the bun. She ate it in one bite. Then she sat at Julie's side.

"I told you not to feed her from the table, Julie. That teaches her to beg, and a begging dog is a nuisance." Mamma's voice was stern. "Please don't do it again."

"That was a good meal." Daddy smiled and pushed his empty plate forward. "Well, now, what about you, Mikey?"

"Huh?" said Mikey.

"What are you learning in school?"

"I'm doing a research project."

"Oh?" Daddy rubbed his chin. "A research project in fourth grade? What happened to good old learning about fractions and geography and all those things?"

"We're going to do fractions," said Mikey. "After

I do ships. But I didn't want to do ships. That's why I'm trying to do something with pirates—to make it more interesting. Pirates are great. I wanted to do guns." Mikey looked quickly at Mamma, who was looking at him with a blank face. "Or cooking. Chinese cooking. Baked cucumbers. I bet I could have won an Olympic medal for them. But Bill checked out my books."

Everyone looked at Mikey in silence for a moment.

"You don't need a secret code," said Victoria. "No one can understand you anyway. You talk like a madman."

Mikey looked right at Victoria. "Kpok," he said. "Kpok, kpok, kpok."

"What . . ." began Daddy.

"Wait," said Mamma softly. "Mikey, what were you saying about cooking?"

"Cook, eat." Julie put an onion ring on her nose. It fell to the floor. Yippy smelled it and sneezed. Julie clapped.

"I don't want to talk about it now." Mikey took another helping of potato salad and stuffed his mouth. It had a perfect blend of mayonnaise and mustard. The best potato salad in the world.

Mamma kept her eyes on Mikey. "I like Chinese food, too."

Daddy looked at Mikey as though he was about to try to ask something again. Then he abruptly turned to Mamma. "Where are the pretzels? Pretzels would make a fine addition to this meal."

Victoria stood up. "I'll go get the box."

"Sit down," said Mamma. "They're gone."

"Mamma ate them," said Calvin. "All except the last one. I saved the last one for Mikey."

Daddy rubbed his chin again. "You ate all the pretzels? I just bought a big box yesterday."

"Don't look at me that way," said Mamma. "I like pretzels. So, Victoria, tell us about life at your big new middle school."

"It's good," said Victoria. "There are three elementary schools that feed the middle school, so everyone began the year strangers to two-thirds of the kids. And that means you get a chance to make new friends. I know a lot of cool new people already. I must know at least half the kids in my grade."

"Good use of fractions," said Daddy. "See, Mikey?" Mikey blinked at Daddy. Daddy blinked back. "So, who have you met new in your class this year, Mikey?"

"Bill." Mikey had met a lot of new people this year—people who he'd never been in class with before—but Bill's name popped out of his mouth because Bill was newer than anyone else; after all, he had just moved to town.

"The Bill who did something with books?" said Mamma.

"Yeah, Bill."

"Bill Petrow?" asked Victoria.

"That might be his last name," said Mikey suspiciously. Victoria always managed to learn odd things, like last names, and then somehow she'd use that information against him.

Victoria finished her peas and put her fork down. "John told me his little brother Bill was in your class. John's the smartest boy in my class that I know. The rest of the boys are lame."

"I hate that word, Victoria. I wish you wouldn't use it." Mamma took Victoria's empty plate and put it on top of hers. "Are you through, Calvin?"

Calvin shoved the rest of his pickle in his mouth. "Yeth."

Mamma added Calvin's plate to the stack in front of her.

"Sarah had a birthday party in school today," said Calvin. "I'm going to have a birthday party in school soon. Aren't I?"

"Two weeks, Calvin, and you'll be five." Mamma stood up. "We have a special dessert. Julie, do you want to serve it?"

"Cake." Julie climbed out of her booster seat and off the chair. She went to the counter. Mamma handed her a basket. Julie slid it onto the table. "Eat." She beamed.

"Cupcakes," said Daddy.

"They're tiny and cute," said Victoria.

"I love them." Calvin squashed a cupcake into his mouth.

"Julie made them," said Mamma. "All by herself."

"That's impossible," said Mikey. He looked around the table. Everyone was eating cupcakes. No one paid any attention to the fact that Julie couldn't have made cupcakes all by herself. Not even Victoria. Why wasn't Victoria saying Mamma was illogical? "It's impossible," he said louder.

"No, it isn't. I bought a mix and she cracked in an egg and poured the milk and stirred."

"But you're the one who put it in the oven."

"No. I bought these little tins, see?" Mamma took a miniature cupcake tin from the cupboard. "Julie filled them and put them in the toaster oven to bake. I just stood beside her."

"They're great," said Daddy. "Julie's the best little cook."

Julie clapped her hands.

Everyone clapped.

How could they betray Mikey like this? Everyone knew he was the best cook in the family. "I made the potato salad."

Daddy looked at Mikey with wide eyes. "Oh. And it was great potato salad, too. You're a fine cook, Mikey."

A fine cook? Mikey tried to calm himself. He knew

Daddy was just praising Julie because she was only two—and for a two-year-old, making cupcakes was terrific. Daddy didn't really think Julie was a better cook than Mikey. But maybe he thought Julie was a better cook than Mikey had been at two. Maybe by the time Julie was in fourth grade, she'd be making fantastic feasts.

Mikey was stupid to think he'd have won the Olympic medal for cooking. Maybe he'd never win the Olympic medal.

Julie tapped Mikey's arm. She held up a cupcake. Her eyes stared intently from her fat little face. "Eat."

Mikey ate the cupcake. "It's good, Julie." And it was. Julie was a good cook. "Thanks," he said sadly.

Julie clapped.

Swords

The Franklin Institute was on Benjamin Franklin Parkway. That made sense. Mikey fixed the street sign in his mind so that if he got separated from his class, he could ask people how to get back to the corner of Twentieth Street and Benjamin Franklin Parkway. That's where the bus would pick the class up at noon.

The class was divided into groups, which would tour the Institute together. Mikey was in a group with Raymond and Jennifer Snot and Alison. Alison's mother was in charge. She kept looking down at an index card that had their names on it. Then she'd lock eyes with them and say things like "You're Raymond. Oh, no, you're Mikey, right? That's right." After the third time, Mikey wondered if she was all right in the head.

"I want to go through the heart first," said Alison.

Mikey nodded his head in agreement. The thing he

most remembered from the last time he'd been here was the giant heart that you climbed through.

Alison's mother smiled nervously. "Well, if that's what everyone wants."

"I didn't vote for the heart," said Raymond.

"Oh, come on," said Alison. "It's the best part."

"All right," said Raymond. "But I didn't vote for it." He blew air through his lips so they flapped noisily. Then he moved over close to Mikey. "That was a horse noise."

Mikey nodded.

Jennifer Snot sneezed.

Alison's mother handed Jennifer Snot a tissue.

They all followed Alison, who ran ahead, twisting her way through the masses of other kids, to the heart. Mikey went up the narrow staircase inside the heart, Raymond behind him and some unknown kid in front of him. There was a continuous flow of kids in front and behind, almost like blood cells coursing through the four chambers of the heart. Pump whoosh whoosh.

As Mikey came out of the heart, Bill bumped into him. "This is boring." He held his Olympic medal out straight from his neck and swung it hard. It circled his neck halfway and flopped on his back. He pulled on the ribbon until the medal hung down his chest again. "Want to go slide the weights?"

Mikey didn't know what Bill was talking about. "No, thanks."

"I passed a demonstration of wave effects on ships. You know, with how much you like boats and all, we should go see it."

Mikey shook his head. He didn't care about boats; he cared about pirates. He cared about hidden treasures and high adventure and, especially, wild sword fights. He glanced away. Alison's mother was looking around in a frenzy. "I've got to go." He ran and joined his group.

A voice came over the loudspeaker, announcing that the airplane would be taking off in fifteen minutes. That was the simulated flight that Mr. Gaynor had told them about.

"I get to be pilot first," said Jennifer Snot. And she sneezed.

Alison's mother unfolded the floor plan of the Institute. "Okay, I can get us there. Stay right behind me." She marched off briskly, clutching the floor plan with both hands.

Alison and Jennifer Snot held hands and skipped behind Alison's mother. They kept bumping into people and giggling.

Raymond took giant steps behind them, swinging his head to each side. He looked over his shoulder at Mikey. "Horses toss their manes."

The Institute was getting more crowded every moment, as busloads of school kids came pouring in, followed by haunted-looking mothers, and teachers shouting directions. Mikey hurried so he wouldn't lose his group. He followed Raymond's striped shirt, maneuvering his way around the throngs into a large room that had a roped-off stage at one end. "En garde!" came the shout. Mikey jumped. He looked at the stage.

A man and woman all dressed in white and wearing big helmets lunged at each other with swords. Mikey pushed his way toward them. The swords had skinny blades. But they had big, beautiful silver bell guards. Mikey held on to the rope at the edge of the stage. The fencers wore special white sneakers, and their feet moved super fast back and forth in front of him. They had on thick white socks that came up to their pants, which came down to below the knees.

The amazing thing was how quiet it was. There was no clank of metal on metal. Instead, the fencers went back and forth, swords always ready. Then one would jab and the other one would instantly block the blade: jab, block. It all happened in a couple of seconds. Mikey tensed up. His shoulders jerked with each jab. These were real blades. This was a real sword fight. And the real thing was a zillion times more wonderful than he'd ever imagined.

Something caught Mikey's eye. A man sat on the

corner of the stage and waved at him with one hand while he twirled the tip of his mustache with the other. When Mikey turned his head to him, the man lifted his eyebrows and gestured to the fencers with his thumb. He pointed at Mikey, then he pointed at a stack of pamphlets on the stage floor.

Mikey picked up a pamphlet. It read: Fencing Academy of Philadelphia. He glanced at the silent, mustached man. But the man was looking at his watch.

And suddenly Mikey was being pulled backward. He stumbled and turned. Alison's mother had him by the arm.

"Oh, I'm so glad I found you." Alison's mother's voice trembled. For one terrible moment Mikey thought she was going to hug him. He drew back. That seemed to do the trick: She blinked several times. "Now you have to stay near me. The other ones are on the flight and you're missing the whole thing. Alison is in charge of them. She's so helpful." Alison's mother's voice caught. "I didn't know where you were. I was afraid something dreadful had happened." She moved her hands as she talked, and the twisted remains of the floor plan shook from her right fist.

Mikey didn't care about the simulated flight. But he was sorry he'd worried Alison's mother. "I was watching the fencing."

Alison's mother looked bewildered, as though Mikey had spoken gibberish. "Well, we can go wait outside the airplane and then we'll all go together to learn about atomic energy. You want to know about atomic energy, don't you?" Her voice cracked.

"Sure I do." Mikey spoke soothingly. "Sure."

In the next few hours Mikey's group visited exhibits on atomic energy and virtual reality and computers. They studied demonstrations of wave effects and weather reporting and static electricity. They went on a real train that actually moved a few feet, and they played on the world's largest pinball machine, and they got cricks in their necks looking up at the long planetarium show. But Mikey saw hardly any of it. All he saw were the two figures in white dancing back and forth in his head, swords ready.

"Mamma!" Mikey clattered down the basement steps.

Mamma turned around. She held a hammer in her right hand. There was white dust in her hair and eyebrows and all over her face. Her eyes and nose and mouth looked like wet black holes. Her clothes were covered with white.

Calvin stood beside her. He was ordinary colored except for his hands, which were white with dust. He smiled. "Hi, Mikey."

"Mamma, I've got to take lessons."

Mamma rubbed the back of her hand across her nose and mouth, exposing a wide streak of skin in the white background. She put her hammer on the floor. "Lessons?"

Mikey took the fencing pamphlet out of his pocket. "Look at this."

Mamma rubbed her hands on the back of her jeans. They were still grimy. She reached for the pamphlet. Mikey didn't want his precious pamphlet to get dirty, but Mamma had to see it. He let her take it.

"Fencing?"

"It's wonderful, Mamma. They practically fly at each other. They're so fast, like snakes striking."

"Swords, Mikey . . ."

"Swords?" said Calvin. "Pirate swords?"

"It's a sport, Mamma. It's not like a weapon. See?" Mikey pointed at the words on the pamphlet. "It talks about 'the modern sport of fencing' right here."

"I'm surprised at you, Mikey. You're my cautious one. How could you want to take up a dangerous sport like fencing?"

"They wear helmets that have net wire across their faces. And a thick glove on the sword hand. And these neat padded outfits. It's safe. Plus the swords don't look like regular swords. They've got squared-off sides. You can't get hurt."

"They have tips, don't they?"

"Tips?"

"The pointed tip, Mikey. That could hurt."

"No one got hurt, Mamma."

Mamma held the pamphlet in her hand and walked slowly up the steps to the kitchen. "What do you mean, no one got hurt? Did you see fencers?"

"There was a demonstration at the Franklin Institute."

Mamma put the pamphlet on the table and washed her hands in the kitchen sink. She turned the burner on under the tea kettle. "Want some banana bread?"

"I do," said Calvin. "Can I take lessons, too?"

"No." Mamma gave Calvin a dishrag. She watched while he wiped off his hands. Then she put a plate of sliced banana bread on the table. "When are the lessons? How much do they cost?"

These were good questions. Mamma was actually thinking about it. Mikey whipped his arm to the right—now quick to the left—slashing at his imaginary foe. Then he ran to the phone. "You have to ask. Here. I can dial." Mikey dialed the number without even looking at the pamphlet. He knew it by heart.

Calvin stuffed half a slice of banana bread into his mouth. "This is different," he said as he chewed. "Mucky."

"But it tastes good, doesn't it?" said Mamma.

"Yes." Calvin picked up the other half with both hands.

"When Julie wakes up, be sure to tell her you like it," said Mamma. "She made it. And she got carried away and mushed up an extra banana. That's why it's a little wet." Mamma took a bite.

Julie made banana bread. Yesterday Mikey would have been upset by that. But right now he didn't care at all. "Hello," said Mikey into the phone. "My mother wants to talk to you." He held the phone out to Mamma.

Mamma gulped down the banana bread and talked to the man on the phone. Mikey listened intently, but half a conversation doesn't tell much. Mamma hung up.

"So?" said Mikey.

The tea kettle whistled. Mamma got the kettle and poured water over the teabag in her cup. "They have classes for beginners from eight to ten years old on Saturday mornings."

Mikey was nine. "Perfect."

"What about soccer?"

Town soccer was for third- and fourth-graders. They met on the school field every Saturday morning, starting this week. Mikey had played town soccer last fall, and he had planned to do it again this fall. But not now. "I don't care about soccer."

"You loved soccer last year."

"Watch." Mikey lunged past Mamma with his invisible sword. "See? I want to fence, Mamma."

Mamma smiled and sipped her tea, while Mikey lunged over and over, slashing the air. "It costs a lot."

Mikey stopped now. Money—always money. He stood beside Mamma's chair. "How much?"

Mamma picked up her banana bread slice, then put it down.

"Can we afford it?" asked Mikey quietly.

"Well, the man said you could have the first three lessons on a trial basis, just to make sure you really liked it before we have to fork over the rest for the ten lessons."

"It only takes ten lessons to become a fencer?"

"It takes years and years to become a fencer. It's like anything else: You have to work at it. But they only make you pay for ten lessons at a time." Mamma looked steadily at Mikey. "He said it's a sport, Mikey. Like you read. But it's swords. I don't know how I feel about this."

"I won't ever hurt anyone, Mamma. I'll be the best sportsman there ever was." Mikey stepped closer.

Mamma sighed. "Are you sure about this? It isn't easy."

No, it takes years. Years and years. Suddenly fencing wasn't just an idea anymore. It might really happen. The thought of a blade pointed at him—real steel pointed right at Mikey—made him go cold with fear. He rubbed both arms.

But then the memory of those two figures in white, quick and tight and strong, danced again in his head. He couldn't say what it was about fencing that drew him, but whatever it was, it held him fast. He had to be one of those figures in white someday. He had to. "I want to start this Saturday."

"Well, you're in luck. He always lets people in during September. That's when most school kids join. The problem is . . ." Mamma paused. She got up and took a container from the cupboard and put the banana bread in it.

Mikey could hardly bear it. He walked over beside his mother. "What?"

"The problem is that we have to get you there, and it's downtown in Philadelphia near the train station."

"You could drive me."

"I hate city driving."

"Dad could drive me."

"He works so hard all week. He should rest on Saturday."

Desperation made Mikey's chest tight. "If it's near the train station, maybe I could take a train."

"Well, that's a thought. I mean, you couldn't go alone. But I could take the train with you. And that wouldn't be any more expensive than paying for parking." Mamma looked at Mikey with thoughtful eyes. "I can bring Calvin and Julie along, and we can walk around and window-shop while you fence." She tapped her fingers on the top of the banana bread container. "Maybe I can get Victoria to watch them sometimes, too, if the weather's bad." She looked at Mikey. "Three trial lessons. Okay. It's a go."

"Yes!" Mikey hugged his mother hard. "Oh, thank you."

"And now," said Mamma, pulling a bag off the counter, "look what I have." She took out a book, *The Good Food of Szechwan*. On the cover was a picture of a cooked chicken with dark, shiny sauce on it and a plate of white cubes smothered in another delicious-looking sauce. "The woman at the bookshop said this was the best Chinese cookbook. What do you think?"

"I want to make that chicken."

"That's what I was hoping you'd say. You've been making a lot of chicken noises lately. So chicken's exactly what I bought."

Birthdays

On the way home from school the next day, Mikey felt a sense of contentment. Tomorrow was Saturday, the first day of his life as a fencer.

Victoria stood on the porch of their house and scowled as Mikey rode his bike up. "What took you so long?"

"I took the longcut."

"The longcut?" Victoria shook her head in disgust. "Mikey, there is no word *longcut*."

"Sure there is. It's the opposite of *shortcut*."

"If you cut it, it gets short, not long. Be logical."

Mikey had had lessons in logic from Victoria all his life. He was sick of Victoria's logic. "Kpok. What do you care how long I took?"

"Listen, this is Friday. My one afternoon with no homework. I want to spend it at Virginia's house. I can't spend the afternoon doing things for you."

"I didn't ask you to do anything for me."

"Mamma said I had to entertain your friend till you got home."

"What friend?"

"John's little brother."

"Bill?" Oh, no, Bill again.

"He's in the backyard playing catch with Calvin."

"Why didn't you tell him to go away?"

"What? Why would I do that?"

"Why didn't you tell him I died and moved to Hamsterdam?"

Victoria furrowed her brows. "You are so illogical."

"I knew you'd say that. You are so predictable." Mikey lifted his chin in triumph. He walked into the house, put his helmet and backpack in his cubby, and went out the kitchen door into the yard. He was just in time to see Calvin catch the ball. What? Calvin caught the ball! He actually caught it.

"What took you so long?" said Bill.

"I caught it," said Calvin. He was wearing a big pair of sunglasses that slid down his nose. He pushed them up. "Did you see? I caught the ball, Mikey."

Yippy barked hello and jumped on Mikey.

Mikey sat in the grass and scratched Yippy's neck. "That's good, Calvin."

Calvin threw the ball. It bounced halfway to Bill.

Bill ran for the ball and threw it easy to Calvin.

Calvin caught it again. He smiled and jumped in place.

How did that happen? Mikey wanted Calvin to catch the balls he threw, too.

"Want to go rafting?" said Bill to Mikey.

Mikey had never been rafting. Rafting meant water. His stomach knotted. He stood up. "Throw the ball to me, Calvin."

Calvin threw the ball. It hit Mikey in the knee and bounced off into Yippy's jaws. Mikey rubbed at his knee.

Bill wrestled the ball from Yippy and tossed it from hand to hand. "Well?"

"I don't have a raft," said Mikey.

"We only need one raft, and I've got one. I made it myself."

"I'll go rafting," said Calvin.

"You can't," said Mikey. "It's dangerous."

"It's not dangerous," said Bill. "I thought you loved boats. Your research project's on boats, right?"

Mikey didn't feel like explaining why he'd chosen boats for his topic. "Calvin can't swim." Mikey looked at Bill. Bill looked back. He was waiting. Mikey had to say something more. "Where do you raft?"

"In Crum Creek. Our neighbor told my mom that's the best spot around. Unless you know someplace better."

Mikey shook his head. "Nah, I don't know anyplace else." He thought about that creek. It was deep in spots. "I can't go, though."

Bill threw the ball to Calvin. And Calvin caught it again. "Why not?"

"I've got something important to do tomorrow," said Mikey. "I can't risk getting wet and . . ." Mikey searched for a reason. ". . . and maybe catching cold."

"It's too hot to catch cold."

"Jennifer Snot has a cold."

"Jennifer Snot? Did you call her *snot?* Wow, that's great." Bill laughed. "She'll die when she finds out."

"Don't tell her," said Mikey. He gulped. Jennifer Snot wasn't a bad sort; in fact, she was nice. He hadn't meant to hurt her feelings by naming her that. He just wanted to remember which Jennifer was *S* and which was *B* and which was *M*. He had to get Bill's mind off that fast. "You really made your raft?"

"Yeah. It's in my garage. Want to see it?"

Mikey felt trapped. "I've got to take care of Calvin."

"Calvin can come."

"I want to see the raft." Calvin turned the ball over and over in his hands. "Please, Mikey. I'll go ask Mamma."

"All right," said Mikey with a sigh.

Calvin disappeared into the kitchen. A moment later he was back. "We have to be home by six."

"I know," said Mikey. "We always have to be home by six."

They walked down the sidewalk, Bill in the lead. Calvin had Yippy by the leash. When they got to Yale Avenue, they turned left. A couple of blocks down, Bill suddenly said, "Oh, no. Quick. Follow me." He ran into the nearest yard and ducked behind a thick bush.

Calvin and Yippy ran after him.

Yippy barked.

Bill reached out and grabbed Calvin by the arm. He yanked him behind the bush. "Can't you keep the dog quiet?" he whispered.

Mikey scooted behind the bush and put his arms around Yippy's neck. "Shhh, Yippy."

"Come in close," whispered Bill. He crouched half under the bush with Calvin.

Mikey crouched beside them. "What's going on?"

Bill breathed hard. "It's this big fifth grader."

"You're as big as most fifth graders."

"Nuh-uh. Not as big as Hugh."

Hugh? Mikey had heard about Hugh. He was one of the bullies the fourth graders stayed away from. Mikey had never had a run-in with Hugh himself, but Raymond had once. Hugh had called him "shorty" and pounded him on the head.

Yippy pulled her head loose from Mikey's grip. She whined.

"Here." Calvin dug in his pocket and brought out a sandy cookie. He flashed it past Yippy's nose, then held it behind his back. Yippy went around behind Calvin and lay down. She crunched the cookie loudly.

"Good work, Calvin." Mikey leaned out just enough to see the street. Three boys walked down the center holding skateboards. They looked pretty normal for fifth graders until you watched a while. Then you could see something special about them— that ominous way they walked. They were almost even with the bush now. He pulled his head back. "There are three of them."

"Hugh's in the middle. The other two are his buddies."

"How do you know them?" asked Calvin.

"They ambush people."

"Do they ambush you?" asked Calvin.

"Yeah. They slam me up against the school yard fence and laugh the whole time. They pretend like they're playing, so if an adult walks by, they can say it's just a game."

Mikey's heart pounded at the treachery. He thought about being slammed hard against a fence— so hard that he couldn't catch his breath—slammed till he dropped, dead on the ground.

Calvin put his hand on Bill's arm. "Do they ambush you a lot?" His sunglasses slid down his nose. He pushed them back up.

"Only if they see me first. But I'm always on guard. And I can spot Hugh a block away."

On guard, thought Mikey. He remembered the fencers at the Franklin Institute shouting, "En garde." He tensed up as though for a duel.

"Yeah, I thought that was you." Hugh and his buddies came around the bush.

Mikey looked up at them from where he squatted. His mouth went dry.

Yippy barked and bounded out.

Hugh jumped back.

But the boy on his right knelt down and petted Yippy. Yippy wagged her tail. "Nice dog."

Hugh relaxed his shoulders and smirked at Bill. "Some watchdog." He laughed. "You hiding?"

Bill stood up. "Why don't you just go your own way?"

"I'll go where I want." Hugh looked at Mikey and Calvin. "So the new kid's finally making friends. Who're these dorks?"

Mikey and Calvin stood up. Mikey stepped half in front of Calvin. If anyone had to die, Mikey should be first. He was older, after all.

The third boy looked at Calvin. "What's your name, pipsqueak?"

Mikey should speak up. He should protect his brother. He opened his mouth, but no sound came out.

Calvin shook his head. "My name's not Pipsqueak. It's Calvin." He shook his head again. "I don't even like fences. Really. I'll never go near the school yard fence."

Hugh looked confused. He scratched his head. "Bunch of dweebs."

"But the dog's nice," said the first boy. Yippy rolled onto her back, and the boy scratched her chest.

Hugh moved close to Bill and squinted. "Where's your face? All I can see is a wart."

His buddies laughed.

"You're lucky I don't ring the doorbell of the house there and get you in trouble for trespassing. I could say you were taking your dog in their yard to poop. That'd be good, huh?"

His buddies laughed.

"We've got things to do. Catch you later." Hugh pointed at Bill's chest. "Get it? Catch you later."

The buddies laughed again.

Hugh walked back down the yard and out to the street. His buddies flanked him.

Yippy stood up and barked.

"He's going to catch you later," said Calvin. "Oh, Bill, he's going to catch you later."

"Not if I see him first," said Bill. "Anyway, don't worry about it. He mainly just likes to make people feel bad."

Mikey took Calvin's hand and squeezed. He wished he had said something tough to Hugh. He wished he had told him to go away. "Try to forget them, Calvin."

"That's right." Bill walked out to the sidewalk. "Let's go look at my raft."

They crossed the street and went down one more block. Mikey kept looking over his shoulder. He hoped he'd never see Hugh again in his life. Finally they turned up a driveway.

"This is it," said Bill.

Calvin and Mikey followed Bill into the garage. Propped against the rear wall was a wide board with big holes drilled into it. A huge inner tube was attached to the board with ropes that wove in and out of the holes. Bill picked up the board and carried it out to the driveway. He set it down with the inner tube on the top side. "What do you think?"

Mikey walked around it. "How does it work?"

"You have two choices. You can sit inside the tube with your legs crossed. It's like being in a regular tube, just with a board under you. But then only one person can go on it. The best way for two people is to sit back-to-back in the center of the tube with your legs hanging out over the sides."

"But then one person goes down the creek backward."

"So what?"

"I love to go backward," said Calvin.

"You're not going rafting," said Mikey. He pressed both hands down on the inner tube. It was tough and sturdy. Mikey looked at Bill with new admiration. "Did you design it yourself?"

"I drilled the holes," Bill said loudly. "And I made Dad buy the board." He crossed his arms on his chest. Then he lowered his voice. "But my big brother designed it. Everyone always thinks he's smart."

"I have a big sister," said Mikey with sympathy.

"I met her."

"Yeah, I forgot." Mikey tapped the edge of the raft lightly with the tip of his sneaker. "You did a good job drilling."

Yippy sniffed the raft where Mikey had tapped it.

"I like tools. My dad taught me how to use them. So, you want to go rafting?"

"There's no time now."

Bill picked up the raft and carried it back inside the garage. He propped it against the wall again. "How about after town soccer tomorrow?"

"I'm not doing soccer."

"What do you mean? Our neighbor said everyone does soccer." Bill frowned.

"Is this yours?" Calvin appeared beside Bill with a pink plastic rake in his hand.

"It used to be," said Bill. "It's for a sandbox. We have a whole crate of old sandbox toys in the garage. Mom saves everything, no matter how often we move."

"Do you move a lot?" asked Mikey.

"Every couple of years. 'Cause of Dad's job."

"I have a sandbox. And I had a pink rake, too." Calvin swung the rake over his head. "But I lost mine."

"You can have that one," said Bill.

"Really?" Calvin stared at Bill.

Bill laughed. "Really."

"You don't have to do that," said Mikey.

"What do I care about an old rake?" said Bill. "And Mom'll never remember."

"Oh, thank you." Calvin jumped and jumped. "I love it." His sunglasses fell off. "Oh, here." He handed the glasses to Bill. "Thanks for letting me borrow them."

Bill smiled at Calvin and put on the sunglasses. "Any time." Then he looked at Mikey. "Come to soccer tomorrow."

"I can't. Tomorrow I'm going . . ." Mikey felt stupid saying he was going to fencing. Bill would probably laugh. How could someone who didn't have the nerve to even talk back to bullies ever hope to be a fencer? "I'm going somewhere with my mother."

"I'm going, too," said Calvin. "We're taking the train to . . ."

"Tell us something about kindergarten," Mikey said quickly. He had to keep Calvin from talking about fencing. "Come on, Calvin. Tell us something that happened today."

Calvin cocked his head. "What?"

"Did anyone throw up?"

"Not today."

Bill looked surprised. "Do kids in your class throw up a lot?"

Calvin nodded. "And Sarah had a birthday today."

"But she just had one the other day," said Mikey.

"I know. She's getting old fast."

Mikey looked at Calvin's face to see if maybe he was joking. He had to be joking. Only his face was dead serious.

Calvin swung his rake. "And I cut my finger so they made me go sit in the corner and suck it."

"What?" said Bill.

"It's time to get home," said Mikey. "See you later, Bill." He took Calvin by the hand.

Calvin waved good-bye with his rake.

Bill looked confused. He waved back. "Yeah." Then he went around the corner of his house.

Mikey walked beside Calvin, with Yippy leading,

pulling at the leash. "Did Sarah really have another birthday today?"

"She likes birthdays."

"Oh." It wasn't worth talking about. "Why'd you borrow Bill's sunglasses?"

"They protect my eyes. That's what Bill said. That way I can keep my eyes open when we play catch."

So that was why Calvin could catch the ball today—he could see it. What a simple solution.

"Mikey, will those mean boys catch us, too?"

"No," said Mikey. But if they did, what would he do? He had no idea.

"Mikey, Bill's the best thrower, even if he has warts."

"Bill doesn't have warts. They only said that to hurt his feelings. Now let's just walk. I want to think about things." So many things. Tomorrow, tomorrow, tomorrow.

The First Lesson

The train rushed toward them, and Mikey's heart rushed to his throat. The huge wheels slowed and finally stopped. Mikey felt his shoulders drop in relief. He realized he'd been breathing through his mouth like a dog. He climbed onto the train behind Mamma, who had Calvin by one hand and Julie by the other.

"You've got the tickets, Mikey, don't you?" Mamma looked at Mikey's empty hands worriedly.

Mikey patted his pocket. "I've got them."

Mamma smiled. She sat down and bounced Julie on her knees.

Calvin stood at the window. "The train's going again. We're going, we're going."

"Sit down, Calvin," said Mamma.

Calvin pressed his forehead against the window and stared. Mikey knew he had no intention of sitting. After a couple of minutes, Calvin said, "Oh, look how far down the ground is."

Mikey looked. They were on a trestle over a creek. The creek was shallow. It looked better for rafting than Crum Creek.

"Oh, I love it," screamed Calvin.

"Love," shouted Julie. "Love train." She threw her arms around Mamma's neck in a giant hug.

Mamma laughed.

Mikey laughed, too. He hadn't been on the train in a long time. This was exciting. Mikey watched the houses flash by. Everything was right.

"Warm-up time. Okay, cadets, there's your path." The man in the fencing suit pointed around the perimeter of an area of floor marked off by white tape. He was the man who had sat on the stage at the Franklin Institute. The mustache man.

One boy raised his hand. "Hey, mister, when do we fence?"

Mikey's heart sped. Would he hold a sword right away?

The man twirled the tip of his mustache. "Call me Coach." He looked at each of them in turn. When he came to Mikey, he winked. "Warm up first. Run nice and slow." Coach ran in place. "When I yell 'Turn,' you run backward." He ran backward. "When I yell 'Change,' you run the other direction." He jumped around and ran off, straight into the men's changing room.

The cadets looked at each other, dumbfounded.

"That doesn't make sense," said the boy who had asked the question. " 'Turn' shouldn't mean run backward."

The boy reminded Mikey of Victoria, always looking for his own kind of logic. Mikey, for one, was glad they were going to warm up and didn't have to hold swords right away. Still, he looked forward to the thrill of the sword.

They stood there another minute. Then one of the boys ran. They all followed.

Coach appeared out of nowhere and called out, "Change."

At first Mikey didn't remember what to do, but the kid in front of him turned to face him, and Mikey quickly turned and ran the other direction.

Almost instantly, Coach called out, "Turn."

This time Mikey didn't hesitate. He ran backward. "Change."

Mikey spun around and ran backward in the other direction.

Finally Coach called, "Enough. It's time for"— he paused, and his eyes sparkled mischievously— "power skips!"

Skips? When Mikey was in kindergarten, he had loved skipping. And just last year he had taught Calvin how to skip. But in fourth grade none of the boys skipped anymore.

"High." Coach skipped in place, higher than Mikey had ever seen anyone skip before. He looked like a kangaroo. "Once around the area, then on the second time skip two forward and one backward, two forward and one backward." He skipped forward and backward. He stopped and, with both hands, he twirled both tips of his mustache. "Got it?"

The cadets skipped.

"Higher," shouted Coach. "Faster."

Mikey skipped higher and faster. It was like being weightless. It felt great.

"Enough." Coach raised his hands and wagged his fingertips.

The cadets stared. They came forward cautiously.

Coach lifted an eyebrow. He gestured with his thumb toward a line of jump ropes that dangled from hooks on the wall. "Grab yourself a rope and stand in front of those mirrors."

The cadets got their ropes and ran to the mirrors.

"Start like this." Coach jump roped with both feet. "When you feel ready . . ." Coach jumped on his right foot. "After a while . . ." He jumped on his left foot. "Finally . . ." Coach jumped with both feet and the rope going backward. Then he stopped. He looked at his watch. He looked at the cadets.

By this time the cadets knew the routine: When Coach stopped demonstrating, they jump roped madly.

Mikey wrapped his rope around his hands to shorten it. He jumped, both feet together. After a while, he jumped on just his right foot. Then he shifted to his left.

"Enough." Coach pointed at their jump ropes; then he pointed at the hooks on the wall.

The boys hung up their jumpropes.

Coach went to the center of the floor and sat down.

The cadets sat on the floor in an arc in front of him.

Coach put his legs out straight to each side. He set his hands flat on the floor in front of him and walked them outward until his chest was close to the floor. He reached both hands over his right leg. Then over his left. Then his arms made big circles.

The cadets did the same.

Coach stretched one leg straight and forward and the other bent and backward. He pulled on his toes. He switched legs and pulled his toes again. Then he stood up.

Mikey stood up, too. He felt dizzy for a second, they'd been working so fast.

Coach put his hands on his hips. "Looking good." He cracked a smile.

Mikey smiled back. They looked good. He looked good. Wow.

"Next time you're sitting around," said Coach,

"do your stretching exercises. Always behave as though you're in training." He gave a quick nod. "Because you are." He jerked his thumb toward the mirrored wall.

The boys lined up in front of the mirrors in silence.

Coach planted one foot facing forward and the other facing to the side, heels together. "Assume starting position." Mikey recognized the stance from the fencers at the Institute. "En garde." Coach reached his front foot forward, so his heels were now about a foot apart.

The cadets did the same.

"Tiptoe." Coach balanced on tiptoe.

The cadets balanced on tiptoe.

Coach slowly bent his knees. "Advance." He moved forward, keeping his feet pointed that same way.

The cadets advanced.

"Retreat." Coach moved backward, holding the stance steady.

The cadets retreated. Advance, retreat. Over and over.

"Enough." Coach rubbed his hands together. "Judging distance is a key skill." Coach walked to a box and opened it. He took out three elastic ropes. "Who's my volunteer?"

Mikey looked at Coach. Coach was looking right at him. Mikey licked his lips anxiously.

Coach handed Mikey one end of an elastic rope. "Our job is to keep this rope taut." Coach held the other end and walked backward till the rope was tight. "We have to stay within the fencing strip." He pointed at a taped-off area. Then he looked at Mikey. "Advance."

Mikey advanced.

Coach retreated, keeping the rope taut. His eyes never left Mikey's face. Mikey looked back with equal intensity. Coach blinked and advanced. The rope went slack for an instant. Mikey quickly retreated.

Coach laughed. "Good stuff. You're fast."

Mikey flushed with pride.

Coach handed his end of the rope to a cadet. He gave out the other two ropes. The pairs of boys advanced and retreated up and down the fencing strips, keeping the elastic ropes taut.

"Now the one of each pair with your back toward me," called Coach, "that one has to close his eyes."

"What?" said one of the boys. It was exactly what Mikey wanted to say: His back was to Coach.

"Do it. Let your other senses come alive."

Mikey closed his eyes and advanced. He felt the rope go slack. He retreated. There, it was taut again.

"Switch."

What did "switch" mean? Mikey opened his eyes. His partner looked at him in panic, then jumped around to face backward. The next boy over ran in a circle, got tangled in his rope, and fell.

"Stop." Coach waved his arms. " 'Switch' means one guy opens his eyes and the other guy closes his. Got it?"

The boys quickly got back into pairs. Mikey's partner closed his eyes and advanced.

"Keep a steady distance. Be aware of any changes so you know when to lunge." Coach walked up and down through the pairs of cadets. "Switch. Focus on staying relaxed."

Relaxed? How could Mikey relax in that stance, with his eyes closed, going forward and backward on the fencing strip?

"Enough." Coach lifted both arms and wagged his fingertips.

They grouped in front of Coach instantly.

"The best strategy is staying out of attack distance. That's what you were working on today—maintaining a safe distance. Fencing is strategy. And not just strategy with your body, but with your mind. A lot of fencing happens up here." Coach tapped his temple. "You have to get your opponent into a pattern and then you break the pattern and while they're stunned, you attack." Coach collected the ropes. "That's it for today, folks."

"But when do we fence?" said the boy who had started the class with the same question.

Mikey had been totally absorbed in the workout this morning. He hadn't thought about actual fencing at all. But now he looked at Coach with a mix of fear and hope.

"When you're ready."

"Next week?"

Coach shook his head. "Not for a long time."

"Awww. So what do we do next week?"

"We work on gaining skills—speed, balance, aim . . ."

Speed, balance, aim? Mikey was fast—Coach had said that himself. And he had great balance on the bike, and no one had better aim than him at pitching baseball. Mikey already had the three skills they were going to work on. Fencing was going to be the right sport for him. Oh, yes.

"How?" said the boy.

"Warm-up, stretching, footwork, and . . ." Coach lowered his voice to a whisper and leaned forward.

The cadets leaned toward him.

". . . the Zen glove drop."

"What's that?"

Coach lifted an eyebrow. Then he looked away.

"Awww," said the boy again.

Coach came over to Mikey. "A lefty." He twirled one tip of his mustache. "I'll write that down so I don't forget to order you a lefty foil."

"A foil?" said Mikey.

"That's what I teach beginners: foil. The blade is

square and the tip is rubber. Later you can take up épée, too. You'll see." Coach walked away.

Mikey looked around, just as Mamma and Calvin and Julie came in the door. Julie clutched a bunch of wilted flowers in one hand. Mamma looked frazzled.

Calvin ran up to Mikey. "Did you stab anyone?"

"No."

"Don't ever stab me."

The ugly words took Mikey by surprise. "I won't, Calvin. I hope I never stab anyone."

Calvin looked dumbfounded. Then he smiled. "Goody."

Rafting

ll the next week Mikey was in training. He sat with one leg forward and one leg bent back, and pulled on his toes when he watched TV. He maintained a steady distance from the kids near him in the lunch line. He skipped backward behind the bamboo grove at recess—checking frequently to make sure no one was near.

When Saturday's lesson came, Mikey was totally ready. This lesson had the same exercises as the first, plus, of course, the Zen glove drop. In the Zen glove drop one person holds out a glove by the fingers. The other person puts a hand on top of the first person's hand. Then the first person drops the glove and the other person quick tries to catch the glove with that same hand before it hits the ground. Mikey wasn't so hot at it, but neither was anyone else in his class. Except for Keisha. It turned out one of the cadets was a girl.

Mikey loved the lesson. He went to bed happy Saturday night and stayed happy Sunday morning. At noon he sauntered into the kitchen and found Victoria making peanut butter and jelly sandwiches. He picked one up and took a bite.

"Hey! Cut it out."

"Huh?" Mikey looked at the line of sandwiches. Six, counting the one in his hand. "You don't need this one."

"Yes I do. Now I'll have to make another." Victoria laid two more pieces of bread on the counter and went to work.

"You can't be that hungry."

"Don't be ridiculous. They're not all for me. They're for my committee."

"What committee?"

Victoria screwed the lid on the jelly jar. "I got elected to Student Council, and I have to gather the opinions of my homeroom class on what the theme should be for our fall dance. So I set up a committee. They're coming over to advise me."

Mikey didn't know what Student Council was. He wished Calvin was here so that Calvin would ask. "Does Mamma know about Student Council?"

"No. The next time Daddy asks what's new at school I'm going to announce it." Victoria cut the sandwiches in half. She arranged them in a circle on a platter. "And don't you tell before I get a chance to."

"Who elected you?"

"My homeroom class, of course. Lots of kids voted for me."

"Why?"

"What do mean, 'why'? I don't know why." Victoria set glasses on the table. "Well, I do know why John voted for me."

"How do you know John voted for you?"

"He sits across from me and I saw him write down my name."

"Oh. Why did he vote for you?"

"Because I have good handwriting."

"Huh? How do you know that?"

"I asked him. I said, 'John, why'd you vote for me?' And he said, 'Because you have good handwriting.' Just like that."

Mikey remembered how Victoria said he wrote like a monkey. He'd never get elected to anything. Maybe that was good. He wouldn't have to make a zillion peanut butter sandwiches.

"Mikey," came Daddy's voice from the front porch. "Mikey."

Mikey gulped down the last of the sandwich and ran to the door. He stopped short. Bill stood on the steps, wearing shorts and those sunglasses of his. What was Bill doing here? Mikey had avoided Bill ever since Bill had started that thing about his raft.

"Mikey," Daddy called again. He put down the

Sunday paper. "Oh, there you are. Come on outside."

Mikey opened the screen door and stepped out. "Hi, Bill."

"Hi."

Daddy smiled. "So, I hear you're going rafting."

"What? I'm not . . ."

"I worked on the raft all week," Bill said quickly. "I varnished the board and attached the tube with a new rope."

"Rafts need upkeep." Daddy nodded his head. "I was telling Bill about the creek in Iowa that I rafted on as a kid."

"Can I go, too?" Calvin came up the steps from the front yard. He carried the pink rake Bill had given him.

"Another time," said Daddy. "I'll come along, too. But not today. Today's for Mikey and Bill." He rested his arms on his knees and leaned toward Mikey with a nostalgic look on his face. "And you're both dressed just right. Keep those sneakers on in the water. You never know what's on the bottom of creeks."

Mikey looked from Bill's steady, hopeful face to Daddy's dreamy, satisfied eyes. He knew he had to go. He swallowed the lump in his throat. Maybe if Calvin asked again, Daddy would decide to come along. Mikey looked hard at Calvin.

Calvin looked back at Mikey. Then his eyes lit up. "Want to see a magic trick?" He dug in his pocket and came out with a fistful of sand. "I'll squeeze this into a rock." He shut his eyes and squeezed so hard his shoulders shook. He opened his eyes and opened his fist. The sand trickled out. "It didn't work this time."

Calvin was pitiful.

"Keep at it," said Bill. "You'll get it right eventually."

Mikey looked fast at Bill. Was he making fun of Calvin? But he didn't seem to be. He seemed to genuinely like Calvin.

"You better get going if you want a full afternoon of it." Daddy stretched. "Calvin, want to take Yippy on a walk with me?"

"Goody." Calvin dropped the rest of the sand on the porch and grabbed Daddy's hand. They walked around to the backyard.

"Well, let's go." Bill led the way to his house. He took off his sunglasses and put them on a window ledge in his garage. "That way I won't lose them in the white water," he said to Mikey with a smile.

Mikey smiled back hesitantly. That was a joke, right? There was no white water in Crum Creek.

They carried the raft along the sidewalk. "You keep a lookout for Hugh on the right side and behind," said Bill. "I'll cover the front and the left."

"Okay," said Mikey. He thought about what Hugh had said that other day. "Has he caught you lately?"

"Yeah, once. But it was nothing big. Just the usual."

The usual. Mikey's stomach did a small, sick flip. He looked around nervously. No one was in sight. The afternoon was sunny and lazy and quiet. After a little while, it was almost fun to keep watch like that. Mikey pretended he and Bill were a team, traveling secretly through enemy territory, on a dangerous mission. It was exciting—as long as Hugh didn't really show up.

Finally, they veered off the sidewalk and marched across the field to the creek.

"So what've you been doing in fencing?" said Bill.

"How'd you know about fencing?"

"Your father told me."

"Oh. Not much."

Bill stopped and turned to Mikey. "Show me."

Mikey put down his end of the raft. He assumed stance. He advanced and retreated. "It's footwork."

Bill let the raft fall on the ground. He mimicked Mikey, pulling his heels together, one foot facing forward, one sideways. He advanced.

"Not bad," said Mikey.

Bill smiled a little.

"Now bend your knees, like this." Mikey advanced a full circle around the raft.

Bill bent his knees and advanced.

"Good," said Mikey, nodding.

Bill grinned.

"Now rise up on your tiptoes."

Bill got on tiptoe. He licked his top lip in concentration.

Mikey demonstrated again, paying special attention to his balance. "See? It's all a matter of weight."

"Weight?" Bill dropped down to his flat feet again. "Weight?" He shook his head and frowned. "It looks like a lot of stupid exercise to me." He retied his sneakers.

Mikey felt confused at the sudden change in Bill's mood. "It gets us ready," he said softly. "And footwork's fun."

Bill walked into the water, dragging the raft. "Feet don't have anything to do with swords. Foot exercise can't get you ready for anything, except maybe football or soccer." He held on to the raft with one hand. "You made a mistake not to come to town soccer. It was great yesterday."

"Fencing was good, too," said Mikey.

"How many sword fights have you been in?"

"None."

"None? How can you like it when you've never even been in a sword fight?"

"I will. Coach ordered me a special lefty foil. That's what you call the sword, a foil."

Bill fingered his Olympic medal. Mikey had never seen him without it since the day Mr. Gaynor had awarded it to him. Bill slipped the medal inside his shirt. "You left-handed?"

"Yeah."

"Then you better put a bullet-proof patch over your heart."

"Huh? Why?"

"Left-handed fencers die more."

"What?"

"You know. You hold your sword with your left hand and the other guy stabs at your heart. Your heart's on your left side."

Mikey knew exactly where his heart was. It was beating so hard now his shirt went up and down. "I bet you're making that up."

"No, I'm not. I heard it once. You know, if you do soccer, you won't die." Bill stared at Mikey.

Mikey knew this was a showdown. He tried not to blink. "I like fencing better."

Bill shook his head again. "Well, it's your heart." He pulled the raft toward him. "We both have to climb on at once, so grab hold."

Mikey took one end of the raft. The water was cool, but the late September air was still warm. His shoes sank a little into the creek bottom. He felt sloggy. And his chest felt all prickly near his heart, as though something were trying to poke its way through the skin.

"When I say 'Jump,' get on backward." Bill pressed down on his end of the raft. "Jump!" Bill jumped on.

Mikey's end of the raft flew up. And so did he. He fell onto his bottom, his head underwater. He scrambled to his feet.

Bill floated along on the raft, already at least ten feet away. "Are you okay?" he called over his shoulder.

"Sure."

"Well, come on. Run."

Mikey did a splash-run. The mud sucked at his shoes. The water rippled by slowly as Mikey gained on the raft. Then he stopped. Why was he doing this? Bill wasn't even nice to him. Bill talked calmly about the idea of a blade slicing into Mikey's chest, as though he didn't care.

"Come on. There's a surprise ahead. Hurry," shouted Bill.

Mikey watched the raft bob away.

Bill jumped off. "You coming?"

"I don't think so." There, he'd said it.

Bill hooked an arm through the raft tube and pushed his way up the current. "Don't quit." He put a hand over the Olympic medal, whose shape showed clearly through his wet shirt. "It's 'cause I weigh more than you. Hugh says I should go on a diet."

Mikey thought of Hugh smashing Bill into the fence and saying mean things. "I don't think you need to go on a diet."

"You don't?" Bill looked at Mikey as though he was making up his mind. Then he plucked at the front of his wet shirt. "Here, I'll hold the raft steady and you get on first."

"You said we had to get on at the same time."

"Nah. I'm strong enough to hold it. You face forward. I've seen it all before. I did a practice run to make sure we'd have fun." He turned the raft as he spoke.

Mikey hesitated.

"Let's go."

Mikey climbed on. Bill got on behind. They moved, back to back, down the creek. The tube was hot from the sun, and it felt good under Mikey's knees. This was kind of peaceful. Pleasant, almost. They floated a long time without saying anything.

Bill twisted around. "Get ready," he said.

"For what?"

"The rapids."

Rapids? So there really was white water here. Mikey's blood thumped in his ears. "What are we supposed to do?"

"Stay on."

Mikey leaned forward and hooked both arms over the tube. The water rushed faster. It splashed up his nose.

"Here we go," called Bill.

The raft slid down a tiny waterfall right toward a rock.

Bill twisted to face forward, looking over Mikey's shoulder. "Lean left," he shouted.

But Mikey couldn't lean left without letting go of the tube with his right arm. And he wasn't about to let go.

They smashed into the rock and bounced off in a spin. Mikey was facing backward now. They had made it. "This raft really works!"

"Yeah, I know."

The water sloshed in Mikey's face, cool and sweet. He kicked his feet in the rushing water.

"Lean right," shouted Bill.

Mikey's whole body tensed for the impact. They slammed into a rock and flipped over. Arms and legs thrashed everywhere. Water rushed in his eyes and nose. He scraped a knee on the now-pebbly bottom. The current tossed him onto his back and carried him downstream.

Mikey tried to swim to the surface, but the water moved too fast. It raced wildly. His chest hurt. He was drowning! He straightened his legs, hoping to shoot up for a gulp of air, and found himself standing. Actually standing.

He looked around. The raft was turned over on a rock.

Bill came up to Mikey, dripping and grinning. "Great, right?"

Mikey panted. The water was only waist deep. He couldn't drown, as long as he didn't panic. He could zoom along and he could capsize and he could get soaked, and he'd live through it all. "Yeah," he said, amazed at his own words, "not bad."

Bill walked backward toward the raft. "I told you."

Mikey thought about all of it. If he could learn to lean the right way, if he could readjust his weight fast to the changes in the water, maybe the raft wouldn't capsize. And rafting would actually help him learn about balance. He laughed. "Rafting is good practice for fencing."

"Fencing? Rafting is nothing like fencing."

"Yes it is. Want to go again next Sunday?"

"I don't know," said Bill slowly. "I'll think about it."

Strategy

ome on, Victoria, I need the practice. Just try it." Mikey gave Victoria one of Calvin's wooden building blocks.

Victoria held the block and looked at Mikey. "What's a wooden block got to do with fencing?"

"Put it in your armpit." Mikey put a block in his left armpit. "Like this."

Victoria scratched her chin. "You swear this is what you're supposed to do?"

"I swear."

"You better not be tricking me."

"Just do it."

Victoria put the block under her right arm.

Mikey picked up the ball. "We have to hold this ball between us with the backs of our fists and we have to move forward and backward without letting either the tennis ball or the wooden blocks fall." Mikey put the ball in place between the back of his left fist and the back of Victoria's right fist.

Mikey advanced. Victoria retreated. The ball fell.

"You have to back up only a little, so the tension on the ball stays steady. Do you understand?"

"Of course I understand."

Mikey put the ball in place. Victoria advanced. Her block fell.

"Make sure your arm doesn't move faster than your body. You have to . . ."

"Shut up," said Victoria. She picked up the wooden block and stuck it under her arm. "Put the stupid ball back in place."

Calvin sat on the floor watching them. "When I grow up, I'm going to fence with Daddy."

"When you grow up," said Victoria, "Daddy'll be decrepit."

"What's *decrepit?*" said Calvin.

"Too old to move around."

"Oh, no," cried Calvin. "Daddy's going to be decrepit."

Victoria sighed. "No, he's not, Calvin. I just said that because I'm annoyed." She glared at Mikey. "Put the ball back."

Mikey put the ball in place. Victoria advanced. Mikey retreated. Then he advanced. She retreated. The ball fell.

"I hate this, Mikey. Six weeks of fencing and this is all you have to show for it?"

"It's important. Keeping distance is half the job."

"Well, it's not my job. I tried to help you. But I'm no good at this. I'm going downstairs."

"Wait. Let's get some winter gloves to fence with."

"You fence with gloves?"

"Yeah. We try to hit each other with the gloves."

"It doesn't sound exciting."

"It is. And, to give you a head start, I'll tell you something I figured out. The ideal distance isn't just a lunge away. I bet you thought it was a lunge. The ideal distance is an advance and a lunge. The extra space keeps you safe."

"I'm safe if I don't fence at all." Victoria left.

Mikey clutched the wooden block in desperation. Tomorrow at fencing lesson they were going to use foils for the first time. Mikey had to be ready. Who could practice with him?

Bill and Mikey had gone rafting three Sundays in a row, but then the weather got cold. So for the past two weeks they'd played catch. Bill would be perfect for practicing with. But Mikey couldn't ask him. The last time they were together Bill had complained that Mikey talked too much about fencing. And all Mikey had done was try to teach him the Zen glove drop. Anyway, Bill said fencing was dumb. He almost seemed to hate it.

Mikey looked at Calvin. Calvin was blowing on his hands. Could Calvin help him? "Calvin, were you paying attention?"

Calvin looked up at Mikey. "How come when I blow on my hand like this"—Calvin rounded his lips and blew—"it's cool, but when I blow on my hand like this"—he opened his mouth wide and breathed hard—"it's warm?"

Mikey shook his head. "I don't know, Calvin." He put the blocks away and tucked the tennis ball under his pillow. Well, the practice he'd had so far would just have to be enough. And, anyway, at least he was better at keeping distance than Victoria. He smiled at the thought.

Mikey was covered with sweat. The warm-up had been long today. He patted his upper lip with his towel. He couldn't wait to hold a foil. He took a deep breath and tried to steady his wild heart.

Coach went over to the supply closet and dragged out a new carton. He raised both arms and wagged his fingertips.

The cadets trooped over obediently.

Coach handed each cadet a white jacket and knickers and a huge helmet. "This is your official outfit. Bring it with you from now on and change into it here. The shoes haven't arrived yet. I'll give them to you next week."

"Can we put on our helmets now?" asked Zach.

"Mask, not helmet. Sure. See how it feels." Coach jerked his thumb toward the changing rooms.

"When you get back, I'll give you your weapons."

Mikey slipped on the mask with shaky hands. He looked over at his family. All of them had come to see him hold a foil for the first time. But no one had told him he'd get his own fencing outfit today. And no one had told him he'd get his own weapon.

Calvin waved from Daddy's lap. Victoria and Julie rummaged around in the old juice refrigerator. Mamma leaned against a wall. She looked at him with wide eyes. She still hadn't come around to the idea that fencing was a sport. Mikey smiled reassuringly at her. Then he remembered his mask covered his face. So he squared his shoulders and tried to look sporty.

Mikey went into the locker room and changed as fast as he could. He was back in minutes.

Coach handed out foils and gloves. When he came to Mikey, he took a roll of blue tape from the shelf and cut off a short section. "You're my only lefty. You'll never confuse your glove with anyone else's, but the foil may take a while to recognize. So . . ." He wrapped the tape once around the handle.

Mikey put on the glove and watched Coach closely. This was it: his foil. He sucked in his bottom lip. Coach held the foil out to him. Mikey gripped it. His hand fit perfectly into the bell guard. He pointed the long blade up. The shine of the new metal struck awe in his heart.

"Hey, Mike." Coach tapped Mikey's mask.

Mikey put on the mask. He was totally ready.

Coach's thumb jerked toward the mirrors. "Foot-work." Coach stepped back and crossed his arms at the chest.

Mikey practiced his advances. It felt different with a foil. And with that heavy mask. The balance was off. Mikey shifted his weight. There, he had it. Balance was everything. If you were even the slightest bit off balance, you couldn't retreat fast and you couldn't attack fast. You were doomed.

"Enough." Coach twirled the tips of his mustache. He pointed to the targets. Circles of different sizes were painted on them. The cadets each chose a target and went to work.

Mikey had practiced at those targets with just his fingertip before. He advanced with the foil toward the biggest circle.

He missed it. Mikey, who had terrific aim, missed that big circle. This was hard. He looked over at Nick just as Nick hit his target perfectly. Mikey hoped he'd never have to face Nick's foil. He turned to his target and tried again. And again.

"Enough." Coach raised his arms and wagged his fingertips. The cadets gathered. Coach didn't lift an eyebrow. He didn't twirl his mustache. He just looked at them with a totally serious face. Tension crept up Mikey's back and neck. "We'll try with opponents now. One pair at a time. The rest of you, take off your masks and watch while"—Coach looked from one cadet to another—"Keisha and Lloyd fence."

Mikey pointed his foil down at his side and held his mask under his arm. That's what he'd seen the older fencers do.

Keisha and Lloyd positioned themselves on a fencing strip.

Coach took Keisha's foil. He assumed starting position and held the foil point down. Then he swung it in an arc and pointed it toward Lloyd.

Lloyd jumped backward.

Coach tilted the foil to touch his own forehead, then he held it out toward Lloyd again. Then he placed the point on the ground. "That's the salute. Begin every bout with a salute." He handed Keisha her foil.

Keisha and Lloyd saluted each other.

Coach nodded. "The hit area is only the vest. Never aim for the neck or face. Never aim below the waist. Foil fencing is a duel to the death. If you get hit in the vest—the chest area—you're dead."

I don't want to die, thought Mikey.

"Your first priority," said Coach, "is don't get hit."

Right, thought Mikey.

"Your second priority," said Coach, "is hit your enemy."

Mikey gulped. He wondered if Mamma was hearing any of this.

"None of that phony TV stuff, where people try to hit each other's blades. Your goal is to hit the vest. Got it?"

Keisha nodded, silently. Lloyd nodded, silently.

Mikey wondered if maybe all the cadets were becoming like Coach, if maybe after a while none of them would talk like ordinary people, but just nod and gesture half the time.

"Back up some. Okay. When you're ready, begin."

Lloyd stood near one end of the fencing strip. He bent his legs a little and seemed to bounce in place. Keisha advanced from the other end. With a quick lunge, she hit him on the chest.

Mikey flinched automatically.

"Touch!" said Coach.

They all looked at Coach. What now? Was Lloyd dead? Mikey could barely breathe. He didn't want it to be over. Poor Lloyd.

"Usually we go till one fencer has five hits. But today we'll only go to two."

Mikey let out his breath in relief.

Lloyd went back to his end of the fencing strip. He shook his shoulders. He seemed to flap his elbows. All of a sudden he broke stance and charged Keisha.

Mikey's mouth opened in horror.

"Stop!" shouted Coach.

Keisha jumped sideways as Lloyd stumbled to a halt right where she had stood.

"Never run," said Coach. "Remember footwork. Maintain distance. Never let the other guy get in close enough for a hit. Surprise with a lunge, yes, but never with an all-out run."

"Sorry," mumbled Lloyd.

Keisha didn't say anything. If Mikey had been in Keisha's position, he might have turned tail and run. That would have been awful. How did Keisha know to jump off the strip like that?

"Start close to the center this time."

Lloyd went to the center of the strip. He bent his knees and advanced. Keisha retreated. They were close to Keisha's end of the strip now.

"If you make someone retreat so far that they back off the strip, you get a point," said Coach. "It's equal to a hit."

Keisha suddenly advanced and Lloyd retreated. Only Keisha was faster. She lunged and hit Lloyd.

Mikey felt as though he were the one who'd been jabbed. He had to work to keep himself from doubling over.

"Touch," said Coach. "Take off your masks, shake hands, and step off the strip."

Keisha and Lloyd took off their masks. Without them, their heads seemed tiny. They shook hands and got off the strip.

Coach looked at Keisha. "Fast footwork. Did you see that, cadets? Speed is a goal. Especially if you find yourself against an opponent of equal skill."

Mikey was glad that Keisha hadn't been his partner today. Usually he liked her for a partner. But today he wanted someone bad. Someone terrible at footwork and distance and everything else. Someone like Raul. He looked right at Raul.

"Mike and Raul, your turn," said Coach.

Wow. It was like Coach had read Mikey's mind. Mikey and Raul put on their masks and stood near the center of the fencing strip. Mikey swung his foil carefully in the salute, and as it circled his head, he felt a cloak of magic envelop him. He was living his dream at last.

Raul advanced, his foil pointed right at Mikey.

That's when Mikey remembered Bill's words: "Left-handed fencers die more." He instinctively covered his heart with his right hand. In that moment, Raul lunged and hit Mikey on the arm.

"Stop," called Coach. "Mike, what was your arm doing on your chest?"

It was protecting me, thought Mikey. "I don't know," he said. His arm hurt where Raul had hit him.

"If he didn't have his arm there, I would have hit him in the chest," said Raul. "So it should count as a hit anyway, shouldn't it? Shouldn't it, Coach?"

Coach lifted an eyebrow and frowned. "No." He pursed his lips. "Never put your arm up. Parry the attack with your blade, not your body. Then repost immediately—get that blade back on target." As Coach talked, he parried an imaginary attack and reposted. He was lightning fast. "And maintain distance. The best way not to get hit is to be out of range. It's just like our exercises. Footwork and distance."

Mikey nodded. But he knew Coach was wrong: This wasn't the same thing as exercising—when they fenced by hitting each other with gloves. A glove could never pierce your heart. And that's why Mikey's whole body felt jittery. And that's why sweat dripped into his eyes and his blood pumped so hard he could feel it in his temples. And that's why he wanted to be outside in the cool air without his mask, just breathing. Breathing and breathing.

Raul advanced. Mikey felt sick in his stomach. But he retreated fast to maintain distance. Raul seemed to puff out his chest a little. He advanced again. He was close now. Too close. Out of the blue came a surge of energy. Mikey lunged and hit Raul in the middle of the chest.

"Touch." Coach nodded. "Did you see that, cadets? Mike retreated fast. That emphasizes the defense and makes your opponent come in too close because he thinks you'll retreat immediately. But that's when Mike took the attack. See? He had less distance to go. That's strategy."

Mikey's ears rang with the praise. Amazing, unexpected, beautiful praise. Strategy. He hadn't even known what he was doing, but it was strategy.

Coach nodded toward them. It was time to fence again.

Raul stood motionless. Mikey realized he was waiting for Mikey to move first. Maybe he wanted to use Mikey's own strategy back on him. Well, Mikey wouldn't fall for it. He waited.

Raul didn't move.

What now? They couldn't stand there doing nothing forever. Mikey advanced with little steps.

Raul retreated with little steps.

Mikey waited for Raul to advance.

Raul stood there.

Mikey advanced a tiny bit more.

Raul retreated another tiny bit.

They both stood there, stock-still.

This was awful. Mikey advanced with teeny-tiny steps.

Raul retreated the teeniest bit possible.

And now they were close again. And again, out of nowhere, came an undeniable urge. Mikey advanced with a huge lunge.

"Touch," said Coach.

Mikey took off his mask in a daze and shook hands with Raul.

"Good strategy again. Mike took little steps on the advance so his opponent would think he had a little lunge. Then he stepped out big and struck." Coach nodded at Nick and Zach.

Nick and Zach took their places and saluted.

Mikey hardly saw them. It was as though Coach's praise had wrapped him in a blanket and nothing else mattered. Mikey had good strategy. He hadn't planned it, so maybe it came naturally. Mikey had heard of such things—natural athletes. Maybe he was a natural fencer.

"I deserved the first touch," hissed Raul in Mikey's ear.

Mikey looked at him, and all at once he remembered the fear that had made him put his hand over his heart. "I know."

Raul looked surprised. Then he nodded. "Next time."

Mikey swallowed hard. This was what fencing was all about. He'd probably get hit over and over. But he'd learn new strategies and he'd get better. Strategy was the key.

Supper

Victoria spun around in the old desk chair that they all loved because it could go in a full circle. Finally she stopped. "I feel sick."

"Just watching you made me sick," said Mikey. He sat on the den floor with a chessboard. He was reading in a book to figure out how each piece moved. Coach had told Mamma and Daddy that Mikey should take up chess because it would make his strategy even better.

"I want to spin," said Calvin. He climbed up on Victoria's lap and they spun together once around.

Then Victoria got up and left the chair to Calvin. "I have to stop fooling around; it's time for me to make supper."

"Supper?" said Calvin. "I thought you were making dinner."

"Supper's the same as dinner," said Mikey. "Just a fancy name for it, 'cause she feels so important."

"I don't feel important," said Victoria. "I'm doing

a job, so Mamma and Daddy can go out. You're the one who thinks you're so important. The strategist." She drew the last word out, as though it was the funniest thing in the world.

"Kpok," said Mikey.

"I love this chair," said Calvin.

"There's an even better one at school," said Victoria. "In keyboarding class I get to sit in a computer chair that goes up and down. But I'm not heavy enough to make it go down, so everyone has to come over and help push down on me."

"I'd love to sit in a chair that went up and down," said Calvin.

"You will someday." Victoria walked toward the door. "Time for work."

Mikey swept the chess pieces into their box. "I'll help."

"Oh, no, you won't. Mamma said I was to be the cook tonight. You just want to be the only one in the limelight."

"Is a limelight green?" said Calvin.

"I don't want to be in the limelight. I'll do whatever you tell me."

"Okay, then get a can of dog food for Yippy."

"Sure. And I'll even set the table."

Victoria looked thoughtful. "Oh, all right. I guess you can set the table."

"Let's have oatmeal." Calvin jumped off the chair.

Victoria made a face. "No one wants oatmeal."

"I do." Calvin stood on one foot.

"I do, too." Mikey closed the chess book. "I like breakfast for dinner."

"No. I'm cooking. I'll make something good."

"Let's vote," said Mikey. "Calvin and I vote for oatmeal."

"You just don't want me to cook because you want to be the only one that gets praised today for your two big hits."

"I should have lost the first touch," said Mikey softly.

"What did you say?"

"You heard me."

"Say it again."

"Raul hit me on the arm, so it didn't count. But he only hit me there because my arm was on my chest where it wasn't supposed to be. Otherwise he would have killed me."

Calvin's eyes opened wide. "Who would have killed you?"

"It's not real killing," said Victoria quickly. "In lessons, a touch with the sword is called killing."

"*Foil,*" said Mikey, "not *sword.*"

"Foil," said Victoria. She looked at Mikey. "Why was your arm on your chest?"

"To protect my heart."

"An arm can't protect against a foil."

"I know." Mikey looked down at his hands. Then he looked at Victoria. "I panicked."

Victoria nodded slowly. "If someone pointed one of those things at me, I guess I'd panic, too."

"You?" Mikey could hardly believe his ears. "You're never afraid of anything. I bet you weren't even afraid of the fifth-grade bullies when you were in fourth grade."

Victoria knitted her brows. "Are there jerks bothering you at school?"

"No. But some of them bother other kids."

"Well, they better not bother you or I'll kick their butts."

Victoria's words made Mikey feel good. Then he looked at her skinny legs and arms. "Have you ever kicked a big bully really?"

Victoria crossed her arms at the chest. "Actually, no. But it's a matter of attitude, Mikey. You have to feel like you can kick butt. Don't think about size. Stand up to a bully and use your head. Use that famous strategy of yours."

How could strategy put a bully in his place? "I'm going to learn chess," said Mikey doubtfully.

"Chess? What's chess got to do with it?"

"Chess teaches strategy. That's what Coach says. If I learn chess, maybe I'll never have to act dumb or afraid again."

"I know how to play chess," said Victoria quietly.

"You do?"

"I used to play it at Jilly's house. I'll teach you if you promise never to make chicken noises at me again."

Jilly was Victoria's best friend, who moved away last year. Mikey knew Victoria missed her. He stepped closer to his sister. "Thanks."

Victoria gave a small smile. "I suppose oatmeal could be fun. We can put bowls of raisins and walnuts on the table, for anyone who wants to add them."

"And chocolate chips," said Calvin.

"That's disgusting." Victoria walked into the kitchen.

"And popcorn," said Calvin.

"No."

Mikey set the table while Victoria boiled the water for the oatmeal and Calvin filled bowls with walnuts and raisins and chocolate chips.

Mamma came in carrying Julie on her hip. She had on a light blue wool skirt and a big blue sweater. Julie fingered Mamma's pearl necklace with one hand and clutched her rag doll with the other.

"You look pretty," said Calvin.

"That's just what I was thinking," said Mikey.

"Really? With all the physical labor I've been doing, my hands are a mess of callouses and I had to wash my hair twice to feel clean." Mamma set Julie

in her booster seat and her rag doll on the edge of
the table, leaning against the wall. "You can get your
dolly again after you eat, Julie."

Yippy walked over and licked Julie's feet. Julie
laughed.

Mamma scratched Yippy behind the ears. "Are you
sure you can manage things, Victoria?"

"Of course I can. I'm in middle school, Ma."

Mamma nodded, but the worry didn't leave her
face. "The Kirbys are home and they said you could
call if you wanted."

The Kirbys lived next door, and their only son was
grown and off at college. They had tons of worms in
their vegetable garden every summer. Mikey liked
them.

"I won't need to call anyone," said Victoria. "Don't
worry. Just have a nice time with your new friends.
What're their names?"

"Tom and Susan. Susan's nice. I started talking to
her in the grocery line. She noticed the paint on my
clothes. She'd like to have her basement redone, like
I did ours." Mamma looked at the pot on the stove.
"What are you making?"

"They wanted oatmeal," said Victoria. "They're
crazy."

"We voted," said Calvin.

Mamma looked across the table. "With raisins and

walnuts and even chocolate chips." She smiled. "You're well prepared. And, Mikey, don't forget to let Yippy out in the yard a few minutes before putting her to bed."

"I won't, Mamma."

"And put the cover over Dragon's cage for the night."

"I will, Mamma."

Mamma kissed each child on the cheek. Then she took a piece of paper from her pocket and attached it to the magnetic clip on the refrigerator. "Here's the phone number of the restaurant."

Daddy came into the kitchen. "Everything okay?"

"I can handle things," said Victoria. "Leave already."

"Of course you can," said Daddy.

"Oh," said Victoria casually, "my friend said she might stop by later for a little while."

"What friend?" said Daddy.

That's what Mikey wanted to know, too. "I thought you were going to teach me chess tonight."

"I'll teach you tomorrow. Virginia's coming over tonight."

Daddy looked at the box on the counter by the stove. "Oatmeal? I love a good bowl of oatmeal."

"You're all crazy," said Victoria.

Daddy smiled. He took Mamma by the arm, and they left.

Victoria poured the dry oatmeal into the now-boiling water and stirred.

Julie looked around. "Mamma all gone. Daddy all gone."

"That's right," said Victoria. "They're going to have a good time and so are we. You'll like Virginia."

"Want chocolate chips?" said Calvin.

"Chip," said Julie. "Want chip."

Calvin put a handful of chips on the table in front of Julie. "Brock lost a tooth in kindergarten today."

Mikey remembered losing his first tooth. It was in an apple at lunch in first grade. "He's young to be losing a tooth."

"He's going to be rich. He's five like me, and he's going to be rich." Calvin had been in the habit of re-minding everyone he was five ever since his birthday a few weeks ago.

"Rich," said Julie. She stuck a fistful of chocolate chips in her mouth.

"He gets twenty-five cents for his tooth."

"Twenty-five cents!" said Mikey. How could Cal-vin think twenty-five cents was a lot of money?

Victoria put a bowl in front of each child's place. "Blow on it, Julie. Blow with me." Victoria blew on Julie's oatmeal.

Julie blew hard. Oatmeal splattered across the table.

Mikey looked at Calvin. He expected Calvin to ask his question about why air was cool when you blew with round lips. He wanted to hear Victoria's answer. But Calvin just blew noisily on his oatmeal.

Victoria sat down. "Okay, let's have a conversation. Mikey, why don't you talk?"

"Huh? What should I talk about?"

"I don't care. Anything."

"We're almost through with guitar lessons. We have them every Monday, Wednesday, and Friday. But we're almost through."

"I want to play guitar," said Calvin.

"Blow," said Julie. She blew again on her oatmeal.

Calvin put a handful of raisins in front of Julie.

"Guitar is fun," said Mikey. "And Monday is the last day, so Raymond gets to do his horse imitations."

"What?" Victoria looked at Mikey. "What an absurd thing to say."

"It's true," said Mikey. "He's good at horse imitations."

"But that's ridiculous," said Victoria. "What's the last guitar lesson got to do with horse imitations?"

Mikey broke walnuts into his oatmeal. "Mr. Shankweiler likes horse imitations. He's the music teacher."

"Then the music teacher's nuts."

"My teacher made us taste salsa," said Calvin. "She's not nuts."

"Nut," said Julie. She stuffed raisins in her mouth.

"No, those are raisins, Julie. You know that." Victoria looked at Calvin. "Your teacher gave you salsa? Like the stuff people eat on corn chips?"

"Chip," said Julie. "Eat chip."

"No, eat your oatmeal now, Julie." Victoria put Julie's spoon into her hand. "You had enough chocolate chips."

"And we get to wear costumes on Halloween. I love my teacher," said Calvin.

Victoria sighed again. "Can't we have a normal conversation?"

Mikey thought about Victoria's question. She loved logic and everything normal. But sometimes life wasn't logical or normal. Mikey wanted life to be different and wonderful. So far in school Mr. Gaynor had handed out eight Olympic medals, and none of them had gone to Mikey. But today at fencing lesson Mikey had learned that he was a natural fencer. Yes, that was it: Mikey would change the topic of his research project to fencing. Oh, yes. Now he would have a real chance at the Olympic medal. He could do a fencing demonstration as part of his research project. Everyone would be amazed. "I'm going to win an Olympic medal," he blurted out with loud determination. "I'm going to win for my research project on how sword fighting has changed through the ages. And when the medal hangs around my neck, all of you will be proud of me." '

"An Olympic medal for a research project? Mikey, do you even know what the Olympics are? That's it," said Victoria. "You're all demented. Let's just eat in silence."

The Fort

The next weekend Mikey watched his mother tie her hair up in a kerchief. "You're going to do their basement all by yourself?"

"All by myself," said Mamma with a smile. "It'll take weeks and weeks. And they're paying me." She went out the door, happy as could be in her old jeans and paint-stained sweatshirt. Mamma's friend Susan had hired her and now she was going off, all on her own. How could a mother abandon her family on a Sunday?

Mikey walked through the kitchen past Calvin.

"How do you spell *love?*" asked Calvin.

Mikey took a piece of scrap paper and printed *love* on it. He put the paper on the table beside Calvin and started down the steps to the basement.

"Stop right there," Victoria called up.

"Huh?" Mikey bent so he could see into the basement. "I want to come down."

"Virginia and I are doing something private. No one else is allowed in the basement."

"That's not fair."

"Mamma said."

Virginia appeared at the bottom of the stairs. "Anyway, your name doesn't start with *V*. The basement is for *V*-people."

"Since when?"

"Since today," said Victoria firmly. "Go help Calvin with his stupid note."

Mikey stood up straight. "Who wants to be a *V*-people anyway?" He went back into the kitchen.

Calvin pushed his note forward proudly. "I finished. Look how good my letters are."

Calvin's letters were neat. Mikey couldn't believe it, but they were actually neater than his. "Why would you care? First Victoria, then John, and now you." Mikey walked around the table, his arms flying, his voice rising. "I have perfectly good handwriting. Everyone's crazy to care about handwriting."

Calvin looked up worriedly. "Are you mad at me, Mikey? Don't be mad. Please don't be mad."

Victoria came upstairs. "So, how do I look?"

Mikey and Calvin stared. Victoria's hair was cut short, right below the ears. Her long braid was gone!

"Virginia did it for me. Well?"

Calvin smiled. "You look just like Mikey."

"Like Mikey!" Victoria gasped and shook her head. "No, I don't. How could you say such a thing, Calvin? How could you?" She ran back down the basement stairs.

"What did I do?" Calvin was practically in tears. "What did I do, Mikey?"

"She doesn't want to look like me."

"Why not? You look good. Why's everyone mad at me all of a sudden?"

The front doorbell rang. Mikey ran to answer it.

A woman smiled at him. "I'm Brock's mother. Is Calvin ready?"

"I'm ready." Calvin came racing from the kitchen. "I'm ready." He flew past Mikey with a wave. "I'm going to Brock's house. You can tell me why everyone's mad later."

Brock's mother looked at Mikey quizzically.

Mikey flashed her a quick smile. He watched as Calvin climbed into the car and it pulled out of the driveway.

Calvin waved again and shouted, "Bye, Mikey, bye."

Mikey stood on the front porch and looked down the road. No one was in sight. A peal of laughter came up from the basement. Mikey felt cold and alone.

Well, so what? He had plenty to do. He could go in the backyard and practice fencing exercises. He walked quickly around the side of the house.

Daddy stood by the kitchen door, looking up at the gutters. He pointed at a joint. "If I change the angle a little, the rain will get channeled over to here." He tapped his shoe on a spot on the ground. "What do you think, Mikey?"

"I think the gutters look good the way they are, Dad."

"We don't want an ice slick near the door like we had last winter. So that's what I'll do." Daddy picked up a pad of paper from the ground and drew a design. He rubbed his chin and mumbled.

Julie pressed leaves on Yippy's back. "Leaf for ween," she said happily to Mikey. Julie had been talking about Halloween ever since the family discussion about costumes at dinner last night.

"Leaves won't stick to fur," said Mikey.

Julie seemed to think about that. "Okay." She pulled off her shirt. Then she wrestled it over Yippy's head.

Yippy stood up. Julie's shirt hung around the dog's neck in a clump.

"Come, baby dog," said Julie. She went to the door. "Help, Mikey."

Mikey opened the door.

"Socks," said Julie happily. She went inside, followed by Yippy.

Mikey imagined Yippy with socks on. He smiled in spite of himself. Then he went to the middle of the yard. He stretched one leg forward and one leg backward. He jumped and switched legs. He did that over and over. Then he ran backward in a circle. Then he hopped on one foot.

Daddy came over and smiled. "You seem restless, Mikey. Where's your friend?"

"I don't have a friend."

"What about that boy you went rafting with?"

"That's Bill. He doesn't really like me."

"Mamma told me he comes over to play ball every day."

"Mamma's crazy. He hasn't come over all week." That wasn't exactly true. Bill had come on Monday. But when Mikey told him about holding his new foil, Bill had left suddenly. "He says I talk too much about fencing."

"Maybe you do."

"I don't talk about it half as much as I think about it."

"You probably still talk about it a lot." Daddy clicked his tongue against the roof of his mouth. "Maybe you should talk about things you can enjoy together. Why don't you go play with him?"

"I don't know where he is, and I don't care."

"Oh." Daddy put his pad and pencil on the lawn chair. "I think I'll take Julie and Yippy to the park. Want to come?"

The park was a few blocks away. It was fenced in, and it had swings and a slide that wasn't even as tall as Daddy and wooden animals on huge springs for little kids to ride on. No one over five would be caught dead in that park.

"No, thanks."

"What're you going to do?"

"I'll take my own walk."

Daddy rubbed his chin again. "Well, all right. See you later." He went inside, calling, "Julie."

Mikey slowly walked down the driveway and out toward Yale Avenue. He didn't think about where he was going; he just turned left automatically.

Within minutes, he was standing outside Bill's house. He waited. Who knew, Bill might just happen to come out the door. But no one came out. Finally, Mikey rang the bell.

A woman in a flowery shirt and black pants opened the door. "Yes?"

"I'm Mikey. Is Bill home?"

"Mikey? You're the great fencer, aren't you?"

Mikey couldn't believe his ears. "I've only taken a few lessons."

The woman smiled wide. "Go on around back. He's working on some construction project. He'll be so glad to see you." She waited. "Go on."

"Thanks." Mikey backed off the step. Then he walked around the house. Bill would be glad to see him? Had Bill's mother confused Mikey with someone else? But who else took fencing?

As Mikey rounded the back corner of the house, he heard a hammer. He followed the noise to a shed behind the garage. Mikey peeked in. "Hi."

Bill put down his hammer. "Hi." He looked surprised.

Mikey glanced around the shed. A stack of boards was propped against one wall. "What're you doing?"

"Building a fort."

"Oh, yeah?" Mikey ran his hand along a board. "What kind of fort?"

Bill took a folded piece of paper from his pocket. He spread it out on the workbench.

Mikey looked at the sketch of a small, square building with a pointed roof. "Wow."

"I designed it without my brother."

"It's great. Where're you going to put it?"

"It'll be a tree fort." Bill pointed to a tree in the corner of his yard.

Mikey looked at the tree with longing. "The first crook there, that's a perfect spot."

"That's what I think, too."

"It's high enough that it could be like a lookout," said Mikey. "You know. Like pirates had."

"You like to play pirates?"

"Well, yeah. I guess I was sort of thinking about pirates when I first decided to start fencing."

"Everything's fencing to you." Bill rubbed the Olympic medal around his neck. The ribbon it hung on was dirty and frayed by now. He heaved a sigh. Then he folded up the design of the fort and stuck it in his back pocket.

Mikey tried again. "It could be a great lookout."

"I've stood up there in the tree. If Hugh's any-where within two blocks, I can see him. I can even see all the way into Jennifer M.'s backyard from there." Bill looked quickly at Mikey. "Do you have a nickname for Jennifer M.?"

"Jennifer Mouth."

"Oh." Bill looked stumped. "Why?"

"She has a mouth."

"So does everyone."

Mikey smiled. "So tell me it's not logical. My sister says I'm not logical all the time. I don't care."

Bill gave a small laugh. "I don't care what my brother says, either." He picked up the hammer and pounded a nail halfway into a board. The head stuck out about an inch. Then he pounded a second one in beside it, the same way.

"Why are you leaving the nails sticking halfway out?"

"I do this to all the boards. I put a couple of nails near each end, like these. Then when I go to hammer the boards to something, I don't have to worry about trying to hold the nails in place. All I have to do is hold the board in place and the nails are ready."

"Good system." Mikey nodded appreciatively. Then he searched the shelves with his eyes. He spied another hammer. He walked over and picked it up. "You going to build it all alone?" He stood beside Bill at the workbench.

Bill looked at the hammer in Mikey's hand. He put another board on the bench and marked two spots near each end with a pencil. Then he shoved the board over in front of Mikey. "I could use some help."

Mikey took a nail and held it in place with his right hand. He swung at it and hit his thumb. Tears stung his eyes.

"It takes a while to get the hang of it."

"I have an idea." Mikey picked up the nail again. His thumb throbbed, but he held the nail steady. This time he tapped lightly. It stuck. He tapped again and again, until the head stuck out about the same amount that Bill's nails stuck out.

"I never saw anyone hammer like that," said Bill.

"Strategy," said Mikey. "You pound. I tap. But the nail gets in either way. Like in fencing. Fencing strategy is . . ."

"I don't want to hear about fencing strategy. I don't want to hear about fencing anything. I told you that." Bill put a box of nails between them. "Let's see who can get the most nails in place the fastest. Ready?"

Mikey gripped his hammer tight. "All right, but only if we can have a second contest, and I get to choose what."

"I don't fence," said Bill.

"It won't be fencing. It'll be . . . chess."

"Chess?"

Victoria had taught Mikey the moves last Sunday, and he'd played with her every night this week. He'd won one game so far, and that may have been only because Victoria got a phone call in the middle and seemed to lose her sense of concentration. Probably he wasn't good enough to beat Bill. But he had to challenge Bill to something, and he couldn't think of anything else. "Know how to play?"

"A little."

"Then we're even. I know a little hammering, you know a little chess. Deal?"

"Deal."

Rules and Rulers

Raymond stood in front of the class and held a poster about horses pulling plows. His research project was on how people's use of horses had changed over the years. It was a good project, but Mikey knew Raymond couldn't win this week's Olympic medal. He had won last week's medal because of his horse imitations during guitar lesson, and no one yet had won two medals. Mikey was sure that Mr. Gaynor would let everyone in the class win one Olympic medal before he let anyone win a second one.

Mikey drummed his fingers on his desk.

Alison tapped him on the shoulder from behind. "Shhh!"

Mikey stopped drumming and moved his knees out and together, out and together. His project was next. They'd been having project presentations during the last half hour of school all week, and now it was Thursday and Mikey knew his project could beat any of the ones he had seen so far. He had notes on index cards, like everyone else. And he had a poster, like everyone else. But he also had something no one else had: a real exhibit. Daddy had dropped Mikey off at school this morning with his fencing bag. In it were his knickers; his jacket; his mask; his fencing shoes; and, best of all, his foil. He was amazed when Mamma had said he could bring his foil. There was a hitch, though. He was allowed to show all that stuff, but he had had to promise that if he did a demonstration, he would use a ruler instead of his foil in the classroom. Mamma was adamant about it. A stupid little plastic ruler. But it didn't matter. Everyone would be impressed with the foil.

Raymond finished talking and took his seat.

"Your turn, Mikey," said Mr. Gaynor.

Mikey lifted the lid of his desk and pulled out his poster. He flattened out the folds and went up to the front of the room. "My project is on swords." He held up the poster and showed the class his drawings. "These swords here"—he pointed to the thick, wide blades—"were used for hacking people apart in wars. They're so heavy, you had to hold them with two hands." Mikey looked around the class.

All eyes were glued to his poster.

"Only knights in the Crusades used the two-handed swords, because they were expensive to make and ordinary people couldn't afford them."

Pete sat in the back of the room and gripped an imaginary sword with both hands. He slashed the air again and again. Mikey smiled at him.

"And these are rapiers. They're lighter and thinner. They used them for duels. Like in Spain and France and Italy." Mikey pointed lower. "These short, heavy ones are cutlasses. They're for chopping at your enemy."

"Those are the kinds pirates used," said Jennifer Snot. She smiled sweetly at Mikey. Then she pulled a handkerchief out of her desk and blew her nose.

Mikey flushed. "That's right."

"Pirates!" Pete hit Stephen on the arm. Stephen turned to Pete, and they did an imaginary duel in the air, complete with cries of rage and pain. By this time most of the class's eyes had turned to the back of the room.

"Pay attention back there," said Mr. Gaynor. He cleared his throat. "Go on, Mikey."

"The ones with the curved hilts are sabers. People fought with them on horseback. And this one over here is a long sword. It's the best kind of battle sword, and it was used through the ages, with the sword in one hand and a shield in the other." Mikey held up the poster so everyone could see.

"But today people don't sword fight anymore; they fence. Fencing is a sport. The two kinds of fencing I know about are called foil and épée. Both of them are duels. That means it's just you and your opponent." Mikey pointed to the poster. "This is an épée blade. See how it's thick and triangular? The duel in épée is to the first blood. So if you knick your opponent before your opponent stabs you, then you get the point. And you can hit anywhere, on the chest or leg or even the hand. That's why the bell guard is so big, to protect your hand, because your hand's a target."

A few heads in the class were nodding as if in agreement. Everyone was paying attention again now.

"Foil uses a different blade, but I didn't draw one."

Pete groaned.

"I brought one."

Pete stood up. "Wow!"

"Sit down, Pete," said Mr. Gaynor.

Mikey grinned. He went to the closet in the corner where Mr. Gaynor had told him to stash his fencing bag until his turn to present his project. He took out the black bag and unzipped it. "These are knickers. They go down to just below your knees. And this is the jacket. See how it's thick all over, to protect you? And these are the official shoes. They look a lot like normal sneakers, but they're lighter, so you can move fast. And this"—Mikey put on his mask—"this is my mask."

Everyone laughed.

"You look like a spaceman," said Raymond.

"You look like one of those guys that go underwater," said Alison.

Mikey took off his mask. "And this is a foil." He pulled out the blade.

Everyone stared.

"See how the blade is square? In foil fencing, the duel is to the death."

Everyone gasped.

"That just means you have to hit someone on the vest area. It doesn't count if you hit on the leg or arm. You have to aim for a killing strike, and you don't get a point unless you hit in the right place. So the bell guard is smaller, 'cause no one aims for the hand."

"Let's see you fence," came a voice. "Give a demonstration."

Mikey looked around.

It was Bill. "Come on. Show us what you can do."

Mikey couldn't tell if Bill meant it in a friendly way or not. Last Sunday Bill had won the hammering contest, of course. But Mikey had actually won the chess game. And neither of them had mentioned the contests since. So Mikey didn't know how Bill felt about the contests—and he wasn't sure how Bill felt about him in this moment, when all he was talking about was fencing. Bill hated fencing. Why would he want Mikey to show the class? But Mikey had planned to show the class a bit of fencing anyway. So it was fine that Bill asked for a demonstration now. "Okay. Let me put all this away first." He stuck the foil in the bag.

"Wait," said Pete. "You can't put your sword away if you're going to fight."

"I'll use a ruler," said Mikey. He took out the ruler.

"A ruler?" said Pete. "How dumb."

"A ruler's a good idea," said Mr. Gaynor. "Otherwise it's too dangerous."

"Well, if he's going to use a ruler," said Pete, "then let me fight him. I've got a ruler, too." Pete held up a ruler and stood in the aisle beside his desk, ready.

"Great," said Raymond.

"Well . . ." said Mr. Gaynor.

"Come on, Mr. Gaynor," said Jennifer Braid.

"Come on," came many voices.

"Okay," said Mr. Gaynor. "If that's all right with you, Mikey."

Mikey had folded his knickers and put them in the bag. Now he stood there with his jacket in his hands and hesitated. "I don't know. There's sort of a lot to it." Mikey kept his eyes down. He didn't want to sound like he was bragging. "You kind of need to take lessons." He folded his jacket as he talked.

"I don't care about lessons," said Pete. "Let's fight."

"Duel," said Mikey. He put his fencing shoes in the bag. "I don't know."

"Wussy."

Mikey looked around. He didn't know who had said that. His breath came dry and his chest hurt. But whoever said that was wrong. Mikey wasn't afraid. No one could get hurt with a ruler. It wasn't that at all.

"That's enough," said Mr. Gaynor. "Mikey's right. You need lessons to fence."

"Awww," said Pete.

The word *wussy* kept whispering in Mikey's ears. Everyone would think he was afraid if he didn't fence. "I guess we could fence a little," said Mikey softly. He'd just go easy on Pete, so that he didn't embarrass him.

"Okay!" Pete ran up the aisle. "Let's go."

Mikey zipped up his fencing bag and stuck it back in the closet. He assumed proper position and held up his ruler. He balanced his weight exactly right. He was poised for action. He hardly noticed all the admiring eyes on him.

Pete swung his ruler in a circle over his head and shouted, "Die!" He chopped at Mikey's left arm from the outside. The pain came in a burst. Mikey's ruler flew out of his hand. Pete jabbed Mikey in the chest. "I killed you!"

"Ha!" said Stephen. "Pete won! How many lessons did you have, Mikey?"

Mikey picked up his ruler and blinked hard. It had all happened so fast he had trouble believing it. His face was hot and his head buzzed and the place where Pete had chopped his arm hurt horribly. He wanted to run away. He wanted to run away and never come back. "You didn't fence by the rules," he said in a half daze.

"I stabbed you in the heart. I killed you. So I won," said Pete. "Those are the rules, right?"

"You're supposed to hit in the vest area and watch your footwork and position and . . ." Mikey looked at Pete. Pete looked at him hard. Everyone was looking at him hard. It was no use. No one would understand. ". . . things like that." Mikey swallowed. "It doesn't matter. You won." He held out his hand to shake.

Pete looked at Mikey's hand in wonder. Then he slapped it. "Hurrah for me."

"Hurrah for Pete," shouted Stephen.

"Hurrah!" came the shouts.

"Okay, there's just enough time for one more project today," said Mr. Gaynor. "Jennifer M., it's your turn."

Special

Mikey practically ran all the way home. He longed for his bike, so that he could pedal faster than ever and get away from everyone. So that he could escape. What an awful day to have been driven to school. He wished Daddy could have left work early and picked him up, too. Anything, anything would be better than having to walk home now.

Mikey kept his eyes on the sidewalk so that he wouldn't have to look people in the face. He had lost the duel. Pete had killed him. So what did it matter if Pete hadn't followed the rules? If it had been a real duel in real life, Mikey would be dead now. Pierced through the heart. Like Bill had said would happen.

Mikey would never win an Olympic medal. And he'd never be a good fencer. That's why he had left his fencing bag at school. He didn't know if he ever wanted to see it again.

The front porch of Mikey's house was empty.

Good. At least Calvin wasn't there to chatter at him right away. Mikey walked quietly through the house, stashing his backpack in his cubby and leaving through the back door. He walked quickly behind the garage. There was his old pile of pinecones, the ones he'd gathered in September. He tunneled a path into the middle of them and lay down on his back.

The pine tree behind the garage stood twice as tall as Mikey's house. He stared up through the needles, looking at nothing. He could hear nothing. He felt nothing. It was almost as though Mikey were nothing.

"Mikey!" came Mamma's voice.

Mikey shook himself out of the trance and sat up. He rubbed at the back of his neck. Then he went inside.

"Oh, hi, sweetie." Mamma and Julie were setting the table. "I was wondering where you were. I wanted to ask you about your big day. But it's almost time to eat now, so you can save it to tell all of us together at the dinner table." She smiled.

Mikey's heart fell. His big day. His catastrophic day.

"Could you get Calvin, please?"

"Where is he?"

"Upstairs, I think."

Mikey climbed the stairs and checked in the playroom. It was empty. He went into the bedroom. "There you are, Calvin. It's dinnertime."

Calvin was holding on to the windowsill with both hands and looking out. His favorite sleep blanket was tucked under his arm. "Shhh."

Mikey walked up behind him. "What is it?"

"There's a cougar in the yard."

"A cougar? A mountain lion?"

"Yes."

Mikey almost said how dumb that was. Then he thought of the voice calling out "wussy" in school today. Mikey had had enough of name-calling for one day. He decided to try to reason Calvin out of this. He looked down at the yard. "Where?"

"It's hiding."

"How do you know it's hiding?"

"That's what cougars do."

"But how do you know it's there?"

"What?"

Mikey shook his head. This tack wasn't working. His brother was a mental case. On the other hand, Mikey understood that kind of worry. In fact, he was surprised that Calvin thought about scary things like cougars. Calvin always seemed so carefree. Mikey felt a pang of sympathy. "Listen, Calvin, if there was a cougar in the yard, Yippy would growl and go nuts. But, see, Yippy's just digging holes in the chrysanthemum bed, like she always does."

"Oh."

"So, see, there's no cougar out there."

"He must have left."

"Sure, Calvin. He left." Mikey closed the blind. He didn't have the energy to talk Calvin out of his crazy cougar idea. He had his own problems. Mamma expected him to tell about his day at the dinner table. He could try diverting her. He could talk about something that would upset her—like that bully Hugh. Mamma went nuts over things like that.

But even if he managed to get Mamma to forget, his problems wouldn't be over. Everyone in the family knew he had brought his fencing gear to school today. So if Mamma didn't ask what had happened, someone else was bound to. Probably Daddy. Daddy always asked that kind of question.

Mikey would have to tell all of them the horrible truth. He tapped Calvin on the shoulder sadly. "Come on, cougar cub. Let's go eat."

"Okay."

Mikey twirled his spaghetti on his fork. Spaghetti was probably his favorite meal of all, but he could hardly taste it.

"So, did anyone have anything unusual happen to them today?" asked Daddy. He looked right at Mikey with a knowing smile. Then he opened a bottle of beer and filled his glass.

Mikey jammed a huge forkful of spaghetti in his mouth, so no one could expect him to talk. It dismayed him how predictable Daddy was.

"We had a standardized test today," said Victoria. She sprinkled cheese in her bowl.

"Oh, poor you," said Mamma.

"No, it was easy. It was about bats."

"Bats?" said Daddy.

"Bat," said Julie. "All bout bat." She jammed her fork into her spaghetti. "Bat bat bat."

Mikey couldn't resist. "Victoria's batty," he said.

"I am not." Victoria tossed her head. She had taken to sleeping with curlers in her hair ever since she'd cut it, and her ringlets bounced now. "We had to read this long thing about bats and answer questions. It was interesting." She took a sip of milk and patted the edges of her hair.

"I really like your hair that way," said Mamma. "It's sophisticated."

Daddy glanced at Victoria's hair; then he looked around. "Could someone please pass me another piece of garlic toast?"

Calvin stood on his chair and pushed the basket of toast toward Daddy.

"Please sit down, Calvin," said Mamma.

Calvin sat down. "Me next."

"So what happened to you today, Calvin?" asked Daddy.

Mikey wondered if Calvin would tell about the cougar and if everyone would laugh at him. He didn't want everyone to laugh at Calvin. He was sick of humiliation. "Tell about kindergarten, Calvin," he said softly.

"We had an assembly about butterflies."

"Oh, how nice." Mamma smiled. "Was the assembly for the whole school?"

Calvin nodded. "Everyone but the people who were absent."

Mamma and Daddy and Victoria laughed.

"You shouldn't laugh," said Mikey defiantly. "Especially not you, Victoria. What Calvin said was logical."

Victoria looked at Mikey. "Yes, but it was obvious. That's why it was funny."

"I didn't think it was funny," said Mikey.

"You'll understand when you're as old as I am."

"I'll never be as old as you are. That's illogical," said Mikey.

Daddy gave a muffled laugh and exchanged glances with Mamma.

"Don't be stupid, Mikey. You know that's not what I meant."

"Mikey," said Daddy loudly, "tell us about your day."

"It's Julie's turn," said Mikey.

Daddy looked surprised. Then he nodded. "Okay,

we'll save the best for last. So, Julie, what good thing happened to you today?"

"Paint," said Julie. She held up both hands, fingers spread. Her hands were red with tomato sauce. "Paint day."

Mamma smiled. "We finger painted. Julie's very good at it. We painted half the morning away. Till Yippy begged us for a walk. But tomorrow we're going to bake again, because Julie wants to make pie."

Mikey stared at his plate the whole time Mamma talked. He knew when she stopped talking, it would be his turn. He had wanted her to talk forever. But now she had stopped. His heart clutched.

"Oh, that reminds me," said Victoria. "Virginia wants to take Yippy overnight tonight."

For an instant Mikey adored Victoria. Please, let her keep talking, please, he said inside his head.

"Overnight?" said Mamma.

"What for?" said Daddy.

"Well, Virginia's never had a pet except a mouse. And it got cancer so they had to have it put to sleep." She shook her head. "Horrible. So she loves Yippy and she wants to borrow her."

"They had a mouse put to sleep?" said Daddy.

"Of course. It's the only humane way," said Victoria.

"Mouse sleep," said Julie. "Mouse sleep. Mouse eat." She put both hands in her spaghetti at once.

"Use your fork, please, Julie," said Mamma. She reached over and put the fork in Julie's fist.

Yes, said Mikey in his head, yes, everyone, keep talking. Keep talking.

"So can she?" said Victoria.

"Well," said Mamma, "I guess that depends on Yippy. Does Yippy like Virginia?"

"Yippy likes anyone who feeds her." Victoria held out a piece of garlic toast to Yippy. Yippy sniffed at it, then took it in her teeth. "See? She's a pig. She'll be perfectly happy at Virginia's for the night."

"I really wish you wouldn't feed the dog from the table. You know better than that, Victoria."

"Sorry. But, anyway, Virginia even bought Yippy a package of cherry licorice sticks, because I told her Yippy loves them. I'll walk her over after dinner."

"You can't go walking alone with the cougar out," said Calvin.

Mikey looked around the table fast. He expected all of them to hoot and howl at Calvin.

"What cougar?" said Victoria.

"Didn't you hear?" said Mamma. "Someone spotted a cougar in Fairmont Park last night. At first they thought it was a prank call or some kind of mistake. But then today there were several sightings, and the latest one was in Delaware County. It's been on the radio all day long."

"Really?" said Mikey. "I thought Calvin was making things up, like he always does."

Mamma laughed. "No, it's true. But Calvin does have a wonderful imagination. It's a gift. It makes him special. Let's all hope he can hold on to it."

Calvin smiled happily. "I'm special."

Mikey stared at Mamma. All of Calvin's stupid little made-up things made him special? The words hit him with a sharp ping of envy. Everything was so easy for Calvin. Things happened right for him without him even trying.

Daddy finished off his beer and sat back. "I can't imagine how a cougar got all the way to eastern Pennsylvania without getting killed by a car. It has to have come from as far as upstate New York, at the closest."

"Maybe it was someone's pet that escaped." Victoria put her fork and glass on her plate and carried it all to the counter by the sink. "Some people are inhumane enough to keep wild animals like that for pets."

"You're probably right," said Mamma.

Mikey thought about how he had spent the afternoon lying in the middle of the pinecone pile, completely unaware of the danger. He looked at Calvin. "You didn't really see the cougar in our backyard, Calvin. You didn't, did you?"

Calvin nodded. "He was hiding."

That couldn't be true. But Mikey shivered in spite of himself.

Mamma pursed her lips. "I doubt that. They said that it's likely to head for the golf course or a park. It'll stay as far away from houses as it can."

"It was far away," said Calvin. "It was in the bushes."

Mamma looked at Calvin and hesitated. Then she turned to Victoria. "Anyway, I'll drive Yippy over to Virginia's house after we've cleaned up from dinner." She picked up the serving bowl. "Does anyone want more spaghetti?"

Mikey put his glass and fork into his plate and pushed back his chair. The meal was over and he'd actually escaped, all because of the excitement about the cougar. He couldn't believe his luck.

"Wait," said Daddy. "We haven't heard about everyone's day yet."

"That's right," said Mamma. "How could I forget?"

There was no escape after all. Dread filled Mikey's throat.

Daddy smiled. "Victoria, come back and sit down. It was a very special day for Mikey. So, Mikey, let's hear about it."

Mikey waited while Victoria sat back down. He looked around the table. They were all looking at him. Julie's eyes were adoring. Calvin's eyes were happy. Victoria's eyes were impatient. Mamma's eyes were expectant. Daddy's eyes were proud.

Mikey's eyes burned. He blinked and blinked. "I can't stand it," he said at last.

Mamma looked alarmed. "What can't you stand, Mikey?"

"I can't stand any of it. Victoria's on the Student Council and I have bad handwriting."

Daddy looked at Mikey blankly. "What?"

"Don't you see? Calvin has imagination. And Julie bakes all the time. And that's all I wanted. I just wanted to be special, like everyone else."

"Mikey, if everyone were special, then it wouldn't be special," said Victoria. "That's illogical."

"Not now, Victoria," said Mamma. She reached her hand across the table and put it over Mikey's. "You are special, Mikey. Very special. Just wanting to do something as unusual and difficult as fencing proves how special you are." She squeezed Mikey's hand. "Did something bad happen?"

Daddy leaned forward. "What happened, Mikey?" he asked gently.

"I fenced Pete." Mikey looked quickly at Mamma. "Just with rulers, like I promised. And . . . he beat me."

"Oh, no," said Calvin.

"Oh, poor Mikey," said Victoria.

"I'm sorry," said Mamma slowly. "I'm so sorry." She got out of her chair and came around the table. She hugged him. "But you know it, Mikey, that's how sports are. Sometimes you win and sometimes you lose."

"But it wasn't fair. He fenced all wrong. He didn't do anything like it's supposed to be done. He broke all the rules."

"Lots of things aren't fair," said Daddy. "You can't control that. What you can do is work and learn and get better at it. Fencing isn't like riding a bike or swimming, where one day you can't do it and the next day you can. It's something you gain skills in gradually." Daddy put both elbows on the table and leaned toward Mikey. "Keep at it. And maybe next time you'll win."

Mikey looked hard at his father. Daddy sounded right. Mikey wanted him to be right.

"Or I could kick Pete's shins in," said Victoria.

"Victoria!" Mamma looked shocked.

"Kick," said Julie. "Kick kick."

"No one's going to kick anyone," said Mamma.

Mikey smiled at his sisters. "Thanks for the thought, anyway."

The Medal

The clock read 2:50. School would be out in a half hour. It was time for the last few research projects. But Mr. Gaynor didn't seem to notice. He had given the class math work sheets and he now sat at his desk, scribbling on a pad of paper.

Eileen raised her hand. "Isn't it time for projects?"

Mr. Gaynor looked up. "Actually, I want you to finish your math now, and we'll have the rest of the projects next week."

"But I was scheduled for today," said Eileen.

"So was I," said Stephen.

Jennifer Mouth nodded her head vehemently, but she didn't say a thing. She clutched a set of index cards in both hands.

"Well, sometimes things come up. Get back to work. There's barely enough time to finish the work sheets as it is."

"What about this week's Olympic medal?" asked Stephen. "How can you give an Olympic medal for the best research project if you haven't seen all the projects yet?"

"You're right," said Mr. Gaynor. "I can't. That's why next week's Olympic medal will be for the best research project."

"So there's no medal this week?" said Pete. "What a cheat."

"Oh, yes, there's a medal." Mr. Gaynor smiled. "There's always a medal on Friday."

"Who gets it?" asked Jennifer Snot.

Mr. Gaynor opened his drawer and held up the medal. It said, "1st Prize—S." Mr. Gaynor cleared his throat. He looked around the room. Then his eyes settled on Mikey. "First prize goes to Mikey, for sportsmanship."

"But I'm the one who won the fight," said Pete.

That was exactly Mikey's thought. He didn't want a medal for losing. He didn't want the booby prize.

"That's not what *sportsmanship* means," said Mr. Gaynor. "Sportsmanship is whether you behave with honor while you play the sport. It has to do with appreciating the sport for itself and not caring only about winning. And it has to do with whether you congratulate your opponent if he wins. For this Mikey earns first prize." He dangled the medal toward Mikey.

Mikey got up while everyone clapped. He took his medal and slipped it into his pocket. Sportsmanship.

It sounded like the sort of thing Mamma would want him to win first prize for—not the sort of thing a kid would want to win. Mikey wanted to win first prize for a skill—for being the best at something that everyone else would recognize as a skill. He sat back down in his seat and looked at Mr. Gaynor. Was that a flicker of pity in Mr. Gaynor's eyes? Mikey looked down and waited for his cheeks to stop burning.

Mikey went down the stairs and out to the bike racks. He balanced his fencing bag across the handlebars and walked the bike slowly. He was taking his fencing bag home today, even though he wasn't sure why.

Mikey reached the first corner and bounced the bike off the curb. His fencing bag slid to one side. He reached for it quickly, and the whole bike and bag and Mikey fell in the street.

"Get up." Bill appeared out of nowhere and straightened Mikey's bike.

Mikey grabbed his fencing bag.

"I'll walk the bike for you," said Bill.

"I didn't know you were here. I didn't see you." Mikey stood up. Suddenly he remembered the word *wussy* when he was giving his project presentation the day before. Had Bill said it? The whole awful event replayed itself in his head. It was all so unfair —the way he'd been led into the duel, the way Pete fenced, the humiliation of it all. Rage filled his chest. "If you think I didn't want to fence because I was afraid, you're a jerk."

"What are you talking about?"

Mikey swallowed. "Well, somebody called me wussy."

"It wasn't me."

"I don't care. If you thought it, you were wrong."

"I didn't think it. I swear. But it was my fault, anyway."

Mikey gripped his fencing bag tight. "What was your fault?"

"That you lost. You wouldn't have even dueled if I hadn't said you should give a demonstration."

Mikey looked at the ground again. "It doesn't matter." What was the point of fighting over it? He stepped on a stick and snapped it in two. "I lost and that's that."

Bill shook his head. "Pete did everything wrong."

Mikey looked up quickly. "What?"

"His footwork was all wrong. Totally. And he hit you on the arm. That's not a fair hit. He only won because he didn't play by the rules."

"How'd you know that?"

Bill laughed. "That's all you talk about, proper fencing form, all the rules and regulations. I know so much it makes me sick." He stood silent for a moment. Then he said, "I'm sorry."

"Thanks." Mikey looked around. The lines were filing onto the school buses, and the kids who walked home were wandering off. Everyone was going about business as usual. But nothing was usual anymore. Everything was terrible. "Now they all think I'm an idiot, taking lessons and everything and not even being able to beat Pete. And they think Mr. Gaynor gave me the Olympic medal because he feels sorry for me."

"No one thinks that. You got it for sportsmanship."

"Sure," Mikey said in a sarcastic tone.

Bill cleared his throat. "Who cares about the dumb Olympic medals, anyway?"

"You do." Mikey twisted the cloth handle of the fencing bag. "You wear yours every day. You got the very first medal of the year."

"I didn't deserve it."

Mikey looked at Bill in astonishment. "Why not?"

"Mr. Gaynor didn't know me yet. It was the first week of school."

"So what?"

"So he felt sorry for me because I was the new kid. He just gave it to be nice. Teachers do that sort of thing. I know." Bill reached inside his sweater and took off his medal. "I hate it. It's a big lie." He threw it up hard.

Mikey watched in horror as the medal disappeared

in a maple tree. He waited for it to come tumbling down. It didn't. The school buses took off down the street, passing under the branches of the big maple. Mikey was sure the rumble of the buses would shake the medal out of the tree. But no. "You shouldn't have done that."

"What does it matter?"

"It matters a lot." Mikey thought about how Bill tucked the medal inside his shirt when he went rafting and how he tugged on it when he was talking. "You deserved the medal for readiness. You're always ready. Every time I turn around, there you are, ready."

Bill laughed. "Are you trying to be funny?"

Mikey spoke fast. He could hardly catch his breath. The pain of Bill losing his precious medal filled his heart. "Look at how you varnished the raft and put a new rope on it so it would be ready. You even pound in nails halfway so they'll be ready. If anyone deserves a medal for readiness, you do."

"Yeah, well, Mr. Gaynor didn't know that when he gave it to me."

"So what? You still earned it."

Bill nodded. "Maybe you're right." He looked up at the maple tree. "Well, it's gone now."

"I can get it." Mikey put his fencing bag on the ground. It made him anxious to let it out of his hands, but most of the kids had already gone home and no one would bother it. Besides, Bill would watch it.

Mikey climbed the tree. The medal had disappeared into the side that hung over the street. Mikey got to the first thick branch in that direction and shimmied his way out.

"Did you find it?"

Mikey looked down. Bill was peering up at him. "Not yet." The afternoon sun glinted off the yellow and orange leaves. With every bounce of the branch, leaves fell. Where was that medal? Was that it, way, way up there? Bill sure had a good arm for throwing. Mikey studied the situation. He could only walk on really thick branches. And the closest thick branch to the medal was more than five feet below it. Mikey couldn't reach that far. He needed a longer arm.

Mikey climbed back to the lower crook and called to Bill. "Pass me my foil."

"What?"

"My foil. It'll give me extra reach."

"Oh." Bill put the bike on its side, unzipped the fencing bag, and passed Mikey the foil. "Be careful."

Mikey shimmied out on the branch again. Then he stood up, gripping a smaller branch on one side, his foil clutched in the other hand. He reached over his head and held on to the wide branch above. He jammed the foil into a cluster of smaller branches and let go of it long enough to swing himself up onto the next higher branch.

"Hey, you're not climbing higher, are you? Get down. The medal doesn't matter that much. You'll fall."

Mikey took the foil in hand again and made his way out on the branch toward the medal.

"Get down. I mean it. I don't even want the stupid medal."

Mikey looked down at Bill's worried face. If Mikey fell, he'd go twenty feet down onto the street and he'd probably break his neck—and impale himself in the process. But he'd been working on balance in fencing lessons for the past seven weeks. If he didn't have good balance by now, he deserved to fall.

And now he was within reach. Mikey slid the tip of the foil through the ribbon of the medal and yanked down hard. The medal didn't budge. That frayed old ribbon was stronger than he'd thought. He worked the foil back and around so that the ribbon was looped around it twice. He yanked down with all his might. The branches shook so hard, Mikey stumbled backward. His breath stuck in his throat. He caught himself and stood on the branch panting, his heart pounding. Then he pulled on the foil once more, harder than ever, and the ribbon finally gave; Bill's Olympic medal fell somewhere below.

"Hey, fatso, that you?"

Mikey looked down. A tall boy came up beside Bill. "You trying to sneak out the front of the school?"

It was Hugh. Horrible Hugh.

Bill's voice cracked. "I'm not bothering you."

"That a new bike?" Hugh kicked at the front tire. "Let me take it for a ride."

Bill raised the bike and stood gripping it by the handles. "Go away."

"I want to take it for a ride." Hugh stood in front of the bike now. "What's this bag here?" He kicked the fencing bag.

"None of your business," said Bill.

Hugh leaned over the bag and put his hand on the zipper.

"Hey," Mikey called down, surprising himself with his own voice. It sounded strong, a lot stronger than he felt.

Hugh looked up. "What're you doing up there?"

Mikey repeated Victoria's advice to himself: Use your head—use strategy. "Hey, Bill," he said, acting as though Hugh weren't even there, "I'm coming down. Get ready to catch my fo . . . my sword."

"Your sword?" Hugh stood up straight.

Bill opened his mouth. Then he shut it. He put the bike down on the ground and stood ready at the foot of the tree.

Mikey climbed down with care. He handed Bill

the foil, then jumped from the lowest branch to the ground.

"Hey, that's a real sword." Hugh took a step back. "What were you doing with a real sword in the tree?"

"Sometimes when fencers get carried away, the swords just sort of fly out of their hands," said Mikey.

"What?" said Hugh.

"Bill's a pretty wild fencer. They don't call him Killer Bill for nothing."

Hugh looked at Mikey. Then he looked at Bill. Bill shrugged. Hugh looked back at Mikey. "Is that blood on your shirt?"

Bill gasped.

Mikey looked down. He must have scraped himself when he stumbled; blood had seeped through his shirt. He tried not to think about it—now was the moment to focus on strategy. "It can take a long time to heal. But every fencer knows those are the risks."

"I've got things to do." Hugh walked away toward the school playground, looking back over his shoulder every few seconds. Then he ran.

Mikey put his foil in the fencing bag.

"Are you okay?" said Bill. "We better get that cut cleaned up."

"It's not as bad as it looks," Mikey said, hoping his words were true. "I didn't even know I had it."

Bill walked to the street and picked up his Olympic medal. "Thanks." He dropped it in his pocket.

The boys walked side by side, Bill holding on to the bike and Mikey holding on to the fencing bag.

After a while Bill said, "I was thinking . . . when you were up there on that high branch, I saw how good you were on your feet. Did you learn that in fencing?"

"Yeah."

Bill chewed on his bottom lip. "You know, even a fencer could fall. Don't climb that high again, okay? Not for anything."

"I won't."

"That was crazy."

"I know."

Bill stopped. He ran his jacket zipper up and down, up and down. "Fencing must be easy for a thin guy like you."

"Huh? It doesn't matter at all whether you're thin or not. Fencers come in all shapes."

"They do? I thought you said weight mattered. You know, when you showed me your footwork the first time. I figured I was too fat to fence."

A light went on in Mikey's head—that was why Bill hated fencing. "Well, sure, weight matters. But it's not how much weight you have. It's how you balance it. You have to balance everything." Mikey thought about Daddy's words last night at the dinner table. He spoke half to himself. "Anyone can get good at fencing. All you have to do is work at it."

Bill took a deep breath and started walking again. "I have soccer every Saturday for another month. But if you feel like it, maybe we could do some fencing stuff on Sundays. I mean, you could sort of give me lessons. Maybe. If you feel like it."

"I feel like it," said Mikey slowly. But did he really? After losing to Pete, he wasn't sure he ever wanted to fence again.

"And then, after a while, when I know the moves, maybe we can do a real demonstration in front of the class. You know, with the right footwork. Following all the rules."

"That's a good idea," said Mikey. It would be a second chance—a chance to set the record straight. Oh, yes. "A great idea."

"Yeah." Bill laughed and shook his head. "Did you see Hugh run?"

Mikey laughed, too. "My sister told me to use strategy. I can't believe it worked."

Bill stopped again. "Let me see your Olympic medal."

Mikey handed Bill his medal.

Bill nodded. "Mr. Gaynor was right to give you the Olympic medal this week. But he made a mistake." Bill slipped the ribbon over Mikey's head so that the medal hung down to the middle of his chest. "The *S* isn't for *sportsmanship*. It's for *strategy*. You've got the best strategy of anyone I ever met."

Mikey's ears burned. "Ever?"

"Ever, in my whole life."

Mikey put his hand over the medal and pressed it against his chest. And he knew now for sure, for dead sure, why he was taking his fencing bag home. Tomorrow he would be at the Fencing Academy of Philadelphia, jumping rope and doing the Zen glove drop and stretching. He would advance and retreat up and down the fencing strips with all the other cadets. He would improve his speed and his balance and his aim and his strategy. All those skills. And the greatest of them was strategy. He smiled. That was what he really loved, after all. Figuring out how to do it and then getting better and better and better at it. Oh, it would be sweet to win, too. Sweeter than sweet. But fencing itself was sweet enough.

30031000208107

F
NAP   Napoli, Donna Jo

On guard

DUE DATE   **BRODART   05/97   15.52**

E⦙   Y